HALF A CENTURY

Gurnam Gill

MINERVA PRESS
NEW DELHI
LONDON MUMBAI

HALF A CENTURY
Copyright © Gurnam Gill 2002
Translated by Sukirat

All Rights Reserved

No part of this book may be reproduced in any form
by photocopying or by any electronic or mechanical means,
including information storage or retrieval systems,
without permission in writing from both the copyright
owner and the publisher of this book.

ISBN 81 7662 265 6

First Published 2002 by
MINERVA PRESS
13 Palam Marg
Vasant Vihar
New Delhi – 110 057

Printed & bound in India
for Minerva Press (India) Pvt. Ltd.

HALF A CENTURY

The views expressed herein are entirely the author's
and no one is to be held responsible
for the same.

About the Book

This is a tale of immigrants spanning four generations. In this account, there is a concurrent portrayal of life in India and Britain.

Most of the characters in this novel have their roots in Punjab. Due to the inadequacy of cultivatable land, many people from the villages of the Doaba region were forced to emigrate in search of a livelihood. Emulating them, some people from other regions also followed suit. All of them had the same aspirations of a prosperous life, and to return home after attaining the means to earn it.

One cannot negate or falsify historical reality. I am not talking of any written history, but drawing from the experience of immigrant life spread over half a century. The reflection of events and characters on these pages can be pleasant and joyous, as well as sad and pensive.

These people, when they left their land, did not leave their heritage behind. While on the one hand, this cultural baggage contained the commitment of familial and social relations, and the ties of friendship and togetherness, on the other, the divisions of caste, religion and bigotry weighed it down. Now, after half a century, most of the superfluous weight from this baggage has been discarded.

These characters, who had embarked on their journey from various parts of a divided land, have come a long way. Today, they are settled in a land where all human beings are treated as equals, their racial and colour differences notwithstanding. All have this same inner conviction.

The third generation of these immigrants feel that global commercial cooperation, and an awareness of universal human values would not allow the outbreak of a third world war.

The fourth generation is quite content with themselves. But you may find them a bit lost probably because when asked, they say, 'We do not know the name of our village or district, though we know that our forefathers hailed from Punjab.'

As a contemporary of the first or the second generation of immigrants, you may find this reply a little disheartening. But when your generation is gone, this sense of belonging is not going to be of much consequence to the younger lot.

Time brings about many changes – this is a universal truth. Time flows constantly like a river. And the life on its banks keeps changing like seasonal crops. Some of us are on one bank of this river called time, while others are across, on the other bank.

This story is no longer restricted to Britain. It has spread over to other European countries as well as to North America. People of Indian origin are no longer immigrants there – they are now citizens.

I cannot tell you more about this book, because the delineation of the events and characters are spread over its pages. Only you will be able to tell me how far I have been successful in mixing the colours of imagination, reality and experience to draw a picture with the sensitivity of words.

Gurnam Gill

Chapter One

As if the wind had changed its course...

Now the ears do not catch the words of love and affection emanating from the confines of this village. Nor does one come across the simplicity and innocent beauty witnessed here earlier.

Mason Bhag Singh and Surjan Singh met each other after a gap of almost twenty years. The passers-by too, after enquiring of their well-being, stopped and joined in their conversation.

'Who could have imagined that one day we would have old people's homes in our village!' exclaimed Bhag Singh, who had returned to his village after having spent two decades in Calcutta.

The voice of the secretary was audible through the loudspeaker of the gurdwara. 'Our first requirement now is to build a "palace". If we build a "palace" in our village, we would not need to book "palaces" in the city to celebrate marriages there. Our money will stay in the village itself. To achieve this, we will have to once again appeal to our brethren in the foreign lands to raise funds...'

'Do not have the same expectations from our foreign brethren. The younger generation is no longer attached to their ancestral villages, and the first generation is surviving on mere pensions. Yes, someone from the second generation may send some money to raise a memorial for his father or grandfather. That too, if his business is flourishing and he has money to spare,' Surjan Singh said in response to the exhortation of the secretary.

Another house has come up on the eastern side of the village, by the roadside. A house that is beautiful – like a hill maiden. The plaster on the sloping, lintelled roof of the verandas has been cut in the shape of tiles and painted red, making it look like a tiled roof from a distance.

A road runs between this newly built house and the house of Baldev Singh. Almost the entire population of the village lives on the western side. On the eastern end, there is just this house and four or five more. Then there is a flour mill and a sawmill. After that, there are fields for miles and miles.

The atmosphere has changed not only in the village of Doaba, but in the villages all over. Neither the inhabitants, nor the crops are the same. Now you can spot unseasonal crops, spreading in the fields like intruders. The sprawling fields of wheat also have corn growing by their side.

This new house, like Baldev Singh's, had also belonged to a foreign settler, Dhyan Singh. A *bhayya* family, of people from the central Indian plains, now lives in this house. Two more *bhayya* families live in houses built in the midst of the fields. These three *bhayya* families together farm Dhyan Singh's land. These days, hardly anyone visits to check the accounts.

When Dhyan Singh's wife Udhee was alive, one could often spot her walking proudly on the terrace. Even Dhyan Singh, walking by her side, appeared taller at that time. After Udhee died, the house remained the same. Seasons changed in the same order, but the void inside him seemed to have dwarfed Dhyan Singh.

Despondency had overwhelmed Dhyan Singh. He tried his hand at many things to fill this emptiness and overcome his melancholy. But then, at times, the turn of events is such that no remedy proves effective…

For a few years his trembling hands bolted the windows and doors of this house, but that too soon became impossible. Eventually, Dhyan Singh was sucked into the grave of his loneliness.

'The parents of people settled abroad used to visit this place occasionally, and some of them will continue visiting for old time's sake. But who knows if their children will ever come to this village! For most of them this place is unfamiliar now. Not merely this place but its people too. Soon they will know no one here.' Surjan Singh uttered these sad words with a sigh.

'Now it looks as if the crops growing here, too, do not know each other,' he continued, looking at the extensive fields.

A few people, engaged in some discussion, could again be spotted in the veranda of the Old People's Home today. Two men from the bus stand came and joined them. The *subedar* appeared preoccupied and spoke in a solemn tone.

'Those who have relatives abroad have started sending their children to English-medium schools. It is Ram Lal, the son of *bhayya* Chanda, who goes to a government-run school in the village. He even ties his hair in a bun on top of his head and covers it with a handkerchief, like Sikh kids,' said the *subedar*.

'Who knows, he might have become Ram Singh (Sikh) from Ram Lal (Hindu)!' said someone, standing there.

'These are the children who will inherit our villages. The atmosphere already bodes that. There is hardly any difference between the cities and our villages now,' added Patwari Kundan Lal.

For a moment, Surjan Singh could see the sun setting on his dreams.

Someone got up and switched on the light in the hall of the Old People's Home.

'Just last year, the land was sold at nine lakhs per acre in our village. And see, now the rate has come down to seven lakhs. Who knows, it may even reduce further to four to five lakhs an acre. I have heard that the price of Sohan Singh's house in the city is also down by one third. And yet, there are no buyers.' Patwari Kundan Lal, true to his professional knowledge of land deals, broached the subject of rising and falling property prices.

'There is so much traffic on the roads now, that one is even afraid of taking a walk.' This voice expressed concern of another kind.

'Like these cars and vans, the aeroplanes are also jinxed now. Earlier, they carried passengers weaving colourful dreams. But now? Now they shuttle passengers with wilted dreams,' Surjan Singh said thoughtfully.

'Maybe that is why Suchcha Singh has sold one acre of his three acres of land for seven lakhs and dispatched his son to America.'

Outside, darkness was beginning to spread like the silence of the mute, and in their minds, like an obscure fear.

Would this fear of the future be justified? It is difficult to say anything. Only time will answer this question.

To be able to look beyond the edge of time is a miracle.

Chapter Two

Baldev Singh had earlier met Cheema and Ravinder a few times in the council baths. Soon they began to recognise and acknowledge each other,.and then started to engage in small talk whenever they met. In due course, this turned into friendship.

A villager who hailed from the same village as Baldev, had assured him that he would get him a job by paying twenty pounds to the foreman, but until now that had remained a mere promise. Maybe similar promises were given by their respective relatives to Ravinder and Cheema too. As of now, all three were still jobless. Then, on the advice of an acquaintance they decided to approach the factories directly and try their luck.

Cheema had taught English in a high school in Punjab. Ravinder had worked as a patwari – a revenue official – in the village. Baldev too had a working knowledge of English as he had spent two years in a college. All three could read and write English, but were unable to grasp the white man's accent. Nor were they able to convey their thoughts in English as they had been to village schools.

They set out from their homes on a Monday morning to try for jobs. There were a few factories located on Ripple Road on the Degenham side. They started making enquiries there.

Often, by the time they approached the gate, the gatekeeper would wave his hand, indicating non-availability of any vacancy there. Then they would hike to the next factory.

At a wood factory, the gatekeeper briskly walked up to

them as soon as they entered. Ravinder suggested that Cheema should talk to him as he had been teaching English earlier. Looking enquiringly at him Cheema asked the gatekeeper, 'Hab ju got any bacancy?'

'Are you looking for a job?' asked the gatekeeper as if he had not heard Cheema's question.

'We want work if there is any vacancy,' Cheema said, enunciating each word this time.

'Oh! Vacancies. Sure, we have,' said the gatekeeper and indicated that they wait in the reception room.

In a short while, an attractive young woman entered the room wishing them good morning with a slightly affected smile, and passed on application forms to each of them. 'Please fill these in. Take your time and I'll be back to collect them.' Having said this, she disappeared into the room next door.

They began filling up the forms taking each other's help.

Baldev said, 'Maybe God will be kind to us this time.'

'What shall I write in the experience column?' Ravinder was worried about the incomplete form.

'What can we write there? Just leave it blank. We have never been inside a wood factory. How can we have any experience? Here too, we have merely seen the gate as yet, not the factory,' Cheema said.

After a while, instead of the young woman, an imposing white man of about forty-five entered the room. They sat up attentively.

'Good morning, gentlemen! May I have your forms please?' he said, and collected the forms from all three.

After a cursory glance at the forms, he looked at them, smiled and asked, 'Well gentlemen, when do you want to start?'

'Cheema, tell him that we are ready, whenever they want us. If they wish we can join from next Monday,' Ravinder prompted Cheema in Punjabi.

Hearing them speak Punjabi, the white man asked, 'Do you understand English?'

'Yes sir,' Ravinder replied like a student in a class.

'We can start whenever you like, sir,' Cheema told the white man in an excessively polite tone.

'Can you start tomorrow?'

'Yes sir,' they replied in unison.

'Don't forget to bring your P45 or national insurance card. I'll see you at eight o'clock in the morning,' he said, and returned to his office.

'Listen, we have not even asked about the pay. Neither the rate, nor the overtime.' Baldev was slightly apprehensive.

'He, too, has not mentioned anything,' Ravinder said a bit baffled.

'Forget it. Why are you worried about the money? There are so many men working here already. The rate should be good. Maybe tomorrow they will complete the paperwork,' Cheema commented.

'I still cannot believe that we have already been hired, without any paperwork. No contract has been signed. In India, sometimes they don't keep their word even after having signed the papers. It has happened to me once. I am really afraid that they may show us the door tomorrow.'

'Who knows! First a woman comes to distribute the forms and then someone else comes to collect them.'

'Maybe the man was the personnel officer, and the young woman his secretary.'

'Well, we'll be wiser tomorrow.'

'Okay. Let us meet at the gate at seven tomorrow. It will be our first day, so it is better to reach half an hour early.'

'Fine, but that is about tomorrow morning. We'll sleep early tonight so that we get up on time. The pubs are open, let us now celebrate our employment,' suggested Baldev.

Shortly after that, they were seen arguing vehemently at the counter of a pub called Eagle Wing. Their raised voices made the whites turn their heads. One of them was saying that he would pay, while the other was insisting that *he* would. The third was blocking both of them with his outstretched arm, and pushing the red ten-shilling note towards the girl at the counter.

After filling their glasses, the waitress looked at them, wondering what their babble was all about. All three had red notes in their hands, and she was unable to decide from whom to accept it.

Each of them had three glasses of bitter that afternoon. They took turns in getting the refills from the counter. No more arguments, like in the case of their first glass, took place. Flushed with their three pints, their already raised voices had risen higher, and they were not conscious of the stares they were getting from other clients. One white man even said, 'Now out, you rustics.'

The following morning they went and stood excitedly at the factory gate at around 7.30. The others coming to the factory looked at them briefly before going in. Some of them had bicycles, some had walked down from the bus stop, and a few had even come by car.

At eight they were handed over to the foreman. First of all, he gave them clock cards and explained how to use those. Then he showed them the canteen for refreshments and lunch, and then the first-aid room.

They were told that they would be paid at the rate of six shillings an hour and that they may work overtime up to three hours. From Monday to Friday, the overtime would be paid at eight shillings an hour and on Saturdays it would be one and half times the basic rate, that is, nine shillings. On Sundays, the overtime would be double the rate at twelve shillings an hour.

When they heard how much they would be getting, they beamed with gratification.

Shortly after that, the foreman instructed the chargehand

to explain their work to them and also acquaint them with the safety precautions. The chargehand gave them a brief introduction and asked them to go to the man in blue overalls, who was talking to someone at the door of the machine room. Pointing towards him, the chargehand said, 'See that bloke in blue? He is waiting for you.'

Noticing that they were looking a bit confused, he again told them that if they did not understand something, they were welcome to seek clarifications as many times as they wanted. They should not feel restrained. These were fast-moving machines and for the sake of safety the workers must know everything clearly.

'Well, if we go on asking repeatedly, he may think that we do not understand English,' said Cheema.

'But what the hell was he saying? I haven't understood anything,' Baldev mentioned frankly.

'I am also not quite clear about this "block" business.' Neither had Ravinder understood what was said.

Since they were talking to each other, the chargehand merely said, 'Are you okay now?' and left them alone.

The three of them looked at each other puzzled. Finally, Cheema spoke, 'Look, those wood blocks lying there. I think he has asked us to pick them up and stack them next to the saw operators.'

They had barely lifted those piles of wood and proceeded towards the sawmill, when the chargehand came running after them, shouting. In response to his shouting and gestures, they put the piles back in their original place. Then the chargehand summoned an Asian called Baig, and explained everything through him.

Baig told them that the chargehand had asked them to go to Mr Smith to understand the safety rules. Mr Smith was the man in blue overalls and the chargehand had referred to him when he said, 'See, that bloke in blue…'

At lunchtime they could not figure out what was there to

eat and how to get it? They stood in the queue for a while and then quit. They decided to wait for Mr Baig so that they could stand behind him in the queue and take the same dishes, as he would pick up.

When Baig did not arrive, they began to look for him near the wall behind the machines. Baig was standing behind the machines with his lunch box of meat pilaff. As soon as he saw them he said, 'Come pals, share my meal.'

'Brother, the problem is that we have never been to a canteen in England before. To tell you the truth, we do not even know the names of these English dishes. We have only had fish and chips until now. So, we do not know what to choose.'

'I hope you eat meat.'

'Yes, we do. But meat surely would be very expensive.'

'Oh no. Everything is almost the same price. There is hardly any difference in prices. Why don't you ask for a pie and chips? That is, a pie with meat and potato chips, and take tea or coffee, whatever you want. Today there is vegetable soup, too. For a measly sum, with free slices of bread. Take that.'

From the second Friday, they began receiving their pay packets regularly, every Friday. Now they looked forward excitedly to the arrival of that day.

In their second pay packet, one of them had three crisp five-pound notes with a red half-pound note. Another one got two five-pound notes and the rest of the money in one-pound notes with a picture of the Queen on them. They began multiplying the amounts by thirteen to find the equivalent in Indian currency. One of them was pleased with his take-home pay of eight hundred rupees, while the other one got a lower amount of seven hundred only.

'Your code number must be lower. I have three children; you have just two. Wouldn't the tax slab change because of that?' Baldev tried to explain the discrepancy to Ravinder.

Now they had become quite friendly with Baig. The foursome would relax together, and always ate breakfast together in the canteen. Lunch, they would most often carry from home. Some would get parathas and pickles, while others would get vegetable, or meat, or egg. In the afternoon they would all share the meals brought with them. When they found out that a shop in Aldgate sold steel lunch boxes, they went there and bought those.

Shortly, they also realised that if they put their lunch boxes on the steam pipes for heating, an hour before lunch, they could eat hot food. Initially, they would buy groceries at Aldgate. Sundays were spent on chores and in watching films. Or they would sit under a quilt, writing letters home and calculating the value of pounds being sent to India by multiplying the amount with the black-market rate of sixteen to one.

Chapter Three

Hari Singh who was from the same village as Baldev, worked in a rubber factory. When a vacancy came up, he got Baldev to join him there. But after joining, Baldev regretted his move a lot.

When he tried to rejoin the wood factory, he was told that his place had already been filled and there was no vacancy.

Now he was stuck in the rubber factory. The work there was dirtier and the pay, less. He would often think of the wood factory which was much better. He would often argue with himself that people like Hari Singh, who were illiterate, had no other option, but why must he work under such conditions. He was not completely uneducated like the others working around him. He was getting even less than before. In the wood factory he made fifteen to sixteen pounds every week, while here he got merely twelve or thirteen.

Ajit Singh always wrote encouraging and consolatory letters to him. He once wrote:

> One has to work hard and endure a lot to get a firm foothold in a foreign country. One has to undergo many hardships. You must not allow yourself to feel homesick. Consider it as a challenge and stick to the place resolutely. If anyone from home writes anything untoward, just ignore that and do not take it to heart. Secondly, try and continue to stay with Sohan. If the work in your factory is heavy and dirty, maybe later Sohan can get you a job in the Ford factory where he works. Old Hari Singh is doing an even heavier job. Since

> you never worked in the village, you must be finding work very arduous. Had you been able to go through one more year of college, you would not have had to undertake such menial jobs.

Whenever his younger brother Nimba wrote to him, it was always to ask for something. In his previous letter, he had entreated him to send a transistor at the earliest. Usually Mindo and Nimba wrote to him jointly.

Most of the workers in the rubber factory were Punjabis. Since they were used to working hard in their fields back home, they did not find this work particularly heavy. To prevent the rubber tubes from sticking from within, they were filled with some kind of powdered chalk as fine as cement. This powder would cover their faces and hair by the evening, but not as badly as in the midland foundries where it was difficult to even recognise anyone.

After completing the shift, they would clean up by blowing compressed air through a half-inch plastic tube on themselves. Then they would pick up their lunch boxes and proceed home. But before reaching home, each one would visit a pub on the way and consume at least two glasses of Guinness Mild. Each newcomer was told that if one did not drink beer, the chalk that entered the lungs throughout the day could cause tuberculosis. In those days just the mention of this disease was enough to scare people.

Although one left the work clothes in the locker and changed into clean ones before leaving the factory for home, yet the body would have a layer of chalk all over. There were no baths in the cheaper accommodations. Hence, there were always long queues in front of council-run public baths on Saturdays. By paying one shilling, one would get a towel and a small bar of soap and stand in the queue. As soon as a bath was vacated, a loud voice would call out 'next please' making the line inch forward. To keep the bath in-charge happy, a tip of six pence was necessary; otherwise one could not empty out the dirty water and refill the bath.

The factory workers would begin to feel relaxed after lying in a wide bath filled with hot water. This hot water acted like fomentation for their exhausted bodies and imparted a pleasant sensation. At times it would even induce sleep. Grime, accumulated over a workweek would float up in the bath – much like scum which comes up when sugar-cane juice is evaporated to make jaggery. Lost in this luxury, if someone overstayed inside, the door would be banged from outside.

Reaching home after work, Baldev checked his letter box. There was a letter from India in it. Paramjit's name at the back acted as an exhilarant. He took the letter and went straight to his tiny room – a boxroom.

Earlier he had shared rooms with many people, sometimes on the ground floor and at times on the first floor. But now he had taken this small room of his own for one and a half pounds per week. In each of the larger adjoining rooms lived four persons. Each person paid one pound per week. Two of the four were on day shift, and the other two worked night shifts. The ones doing night shifts worked from 6 p.m. to 6 a.m., twelve hours everyday but for five nights only. For that reason, over the weekends two people had to share a bed.

Paramjit's letter made him very unhappy. It was the first time she had written such a sad letter.

The letter read:

The writer, Paramjit sends Sat Sri Akal to dear and respected Sardarji.

I did not want to write about this, but neither can I keep it from you. Instigated by the garden owner's son Meeka,

Nimba has misbehaved with me. I cried through the night. The children kept asking me what had happened. What could I say to them? Merely said that I had a stomach ache. They woke up Maji. *I told* Maji *everything but she forbade me to say anything to* Pitaji and Bhaji. *She even asked me not to let you know about it. But I cannot hide it from you. For me, Nimba is like a younger brother.*

He is getting spoilt by the money you send. He and Meeka often go to see films these days. He keeps on playing the transistor that you have sent till late in the night, blaring out film songs. Pitaji *is mostly in the field-hut and does not know whether Nimba goes to study or to cinema halls.*

To tell you the truth, we are no longer able to live alone. I beg of you, please call us to live with you. Forgive me for any slip.

Simranjit, Rashim and Daljit convey their Sat Sri Akal.

Rashim is always looking at the new photo you have sent.

Sat Sri Akal *with folded hands. Please reply at the earliest.*

Consider this letter as a telegram, I implore you.

Your own,
Paramjit Kaur

Baldev read the letter two or three times. He was incensed by what he read and was enraged with Nimba. Had he been there physically, he would have slapped him hard. Then he was overwhelmed with pity for his wife and children. He felt helpless and began to cry. Meanwhile, he heard the door to the adjoining room open, and immediately wiped his tears with a towel. He tried to sit back and look as normal as possible.

Sleep evaded him that night. He recalled Paramjit's forlorn face on the day he was to leave for England. *What a simple and innocent face she has! She is such a simple woman*, he thought, and then, the faces of his children floated before his eyes.

He wished he had spent one more year in college and obtained the engineering degree. Then he would not have had to struggle in these factories.

But what guarantee was there that he would have got a job in India? Being employed in India has its own charm – to be able to return home every evening and enjoy the company of one's family, the sight of wells and fields of one's native village, to play a match of kabaddi with the children at dusk... Many such scenes were replayed in his mind.

He woke up in the morning, feeling tired. Although he left his room on time for work, he did not feel like going to work. He wandered aimlessly in the market for a while, and then proceeded towards River Road.

In search of a new job, he started knocking at the gates of factories and warehouses. After drawing a blank at four or five places, finally he found a job in a warehouse of sanitary goods.

As compared to his earlier job, work here was easier, cleaner and with a good chance of working overtime. In the previous factory, he earned fourteen pounds working from 7 a.m. to 7 p.m. But now he was making even more. His relatives were green with envy, when they heard of his wages. He began to like England a bit. How can you begin to like a place unless you enjoy your work? After all, a man spends half of his life at his workplace.

He had a sister-in-law called Kamala Rani – a distant cousin. Earlier she had been hesitant to even offer him a room on rent in her house, but now after hearing that he was saving up to twenty pounds a week, she had begun to behave very affectionately as if he were her favourite relative. However, Baldev's pride didn't let him.

Once he accumulated a respectable amount of money, he began to think of buying a house. But his educated co-workers and sundry relatives restrained him from doing so, saying that such a move would ground him to this place forever. They gave him well-intended advice. He should try and free himself instead. He should ask his wife to be patient; after all, others had also left their wives and children behind. Someone would cite his own example saying that he had been stuck here for the last ten years. Of course, he was dying to travel home. But what could he do? If he spent money on travelling, he would never be able to save enough and return home for good.

He was still debating whether to buy a house or not, when he received a letter from his father Jagar Singh. His father had written that the land adjoining theirs was on sale by the Roorkee family. It would be very beneficial to them if these two acres were also bought and included in their holding.

As soon as he received the letter, he collected his own savings, and along with some more money borrowed from his friend Sohan Singh, sent the entire amount home through Kehar Singh Dhoot at the black-market rate of sixteen rupees to a pound.

The moment his friends came to know that he had sent money home, they began to pester him to push the money. Whenever anyone sent money back home, it was customary to 'push' that money by treating his friends to beer in a pub.

They went to the pub adjoining the station. Each one had five pints. He spent one pound, and from the other ten-shilling note, got back two half-crowns as the remaining change. Sipping beer, and lost in his thoughts, Baldev Singh visualised the two acres of the Roorkee family which could now be their own holding. Right up to the next pathway, the entire stretch would now be theirs. This thought made his *Jutt* heart leap with joy and he drank some more. People at the adjoining tables threw him dirty looks.

It was very cold. The temperature was two degrees below freezing point.

Which street was this and where? He was with his friend Sohan Singh; both of them were walking side by side. Suddenly, Baldev Singh said, 'My bladder is full. Let us find a spot to pee. There are no public toilets in sight.'

'Let us go towards the park. Maybe we'll find a toilet there,' Sohan Singh suggested.

'But pal, my bladder will burst any moment. I am getting spasms. I cannot wait any more,' Baldev explained his urgency and his helplessness.

'Why don't you pee behind this hedge next to the road. Nobody can see you there,' advised Sohan Singh.

He was about to unzip his trousers when he saw a woman pass by.

Then he tried to pee against the wall of a factory, but felt as if someone from the adjoining flats was peeping out and watching him. He quickly zipped up but two drops still leaked out involuntarily.

A man in a cap went past, staring at him. Baldev looked down to check if there were any wet spots showing.

After surveying his surroundings, he was about to try again when the man in a cap reappeared. The spasms were unbearable now and he could hardly walk. He again found refuge in a hedge to relieve himself, but the man in a cap was there too.

'Oh, thanks, dear man with a cap. God bless you,' said Baldev Singh, getting up from the bed and running down.

That night Baldev Singh had slept over at Sohan Singh's place. While he was going downstairs, Sohan shouted from behind, 'Soil the kitchen sink now. Do not go out in the cold. Look at him running like a sprinter!'

When he returned, Baldev began to laugh loudly looking at Sohan Singh.

'What is so funny? You shameless creature.'

'Not what you are thinking of. It is something else.'

'What else? After guzzling so much beer last night you

are yearning for your wife.'

'No, pal. Had that man in the cap not turned up for a few seconds more, I would have wet the bed,' Baldev Singh told his friend about his dream and both of them burst out laughing.

'First, you carried on guzzling Guinness Bitter and then went off to sleep immediately after eating. Had you emptied your bladder before retiring, such a thing would not have happened.'

'Pal, I really want to thank that man with the cap. Had he not come, I would have wet this bed. Maybe that is why he kept on appearing repeatedly...' The room resounded with their laughter for a while.

'Now go to sleep. God knows what our neighbours must be thinking. We still have three more hours of sleep.'

'Ah! Now I'll be able to sleep in peace,' Baldev said with a relaxed drawl.

Chapter Four

By the time Baldev completed his second year in the engineering college, his voucher – already extended by three months – was about to expire.

'Don't you miss the chance to go to England,' his friend, Sohan Singh would warn him again and again. Sohan Singh had left school while he was in the tenth class, and left for England about three years ago.

The first people to arrive in England were mostly illiterate. Later, between 1962 and 1965, educated people started coming to England against vouchers.

At Baldev's place of work, a handsome Sikh boy, Paramjit Singh Atwal, worked as the foreman. He spoke English with an almost native accent and mixed freely with the whites. He had with many English girls as friends.

He worked in the day shift and attended college in the evenings. On Sundays, he took lessons for an hour in a Flying Club for a pilot's licence. He belonged to a rich family in Punjab, and owned a car and a house.

On Atwal's suggestion, Baldev joined Eastham College. Since he had already completed two years of college in India, he was admitted into the second semester of the second year saving him a year and a half.

After finishing work at 5 p.m. he would barely make it to the college by 5.45. Sometimes he would reach late. He had to go home first, to change, and at times would miss the bus. The ride back home from his college was at half past nine. By the time he reached home it would be 11 p.m. Then he had to prepare something to eat, making it impossible for him to sleep before midnight. Due to exhaustion, he would find it difficult to get up at six in the morning.

Baldev Singh felt that he would not be able to bear this ordeal for long. Atwal comforted him by saying that since he had already managed to pull through the last six months, another year would also go by. He must be firm in his resolve as his sacrifice today would bear fruit tomorrow. But Baldev was exhausted, and told him so. 'Atwal Sahib, our circumstances are different. You are single and free; we are shackled by the encumbrance of a family. We cannot run away from that responsibility. You do not have to send money to anyone back home. You own a house here, and receive rent from that. You have a car and do not have to wait for the buses. You find English easy as if it were your mother tongue... And frolicking with the *mems* is gratuitous.'

'But you know when I arrived here I had merely three pounds in my wallet. Everything else came later. In a few years, you too will be in possession of all this. Do not give up...'

But Baldev Singh had given up. The time he had been devoting to college was now spent working overtime and saving money.

Initially he had written to Paramjit to stay put for another year or two. He had implored her to bear the hardship for the sake of his education, a better job and their future. But now he had made up his mind to buy a house and get his family to England. That is why he was doing as much overtime as possible. He was working day and night to raise money at the earliest for the house deposit and the air tickets for his family.

It was a Sunday. The following day was a bank holiday, so Monday too was off. Baldev had just woken up when his friend Sukhdev Singh Samra knocked at his door. Samra said, '*Shaheed* is showing at Lyttonstone. Let's go and see the film.'

They took the British Rail from Barking Station and reached Lyttonstone in a short while.

Watching the film Baldev recalled that his uncle, Kultar Singh had mentioned this film to him earlier. The producer, Mr Kashyap had needed some information to make this film. He had also expressed a desire to talk to Kultar Singh's sister in this regard. He had heard about this when he was on a visit to Saharanpur with his older maternal uncle.

Until then, Baldev had not seen any film of Manoj Kumar's. Since he appreciated a good performance and was emotional by nature, he was much moved by *Shaheed*. Nationalism was in his veins. To settle down in this alien land and become a part of it started seeming like an absurd decision. He was filled with feelings of allegiance to India, and felt a sudden grudge towards England.

When he multiplied the money he had already saved, by eighteen, the amount came to almost a hundred thousand. The following day he wrote to Paramjit that he was coming to India. God knows why it was very difficult to integrate into the society here. He was finding everything around alien to him.

> *Even if we buy a house here, it will not give the warmth and freedom expected of a home in India. The intimacy one gets from a mere hall and a courtyard in India cannot be had in England. That is why I think that if we get stuck here now, it would be impossible to get out later. If one can ensure good education for the children in India so that they may secure honourable jobs, there is no need for us to suffer in a foreign land.*
>
> *I know that you must have woven colourful dreams about life in England and my letter is bound to disappoint you. But*

you have only heard of England, not experienced the life here. Even the flowers here are like paper flowers, without any fragrance.

I shall inform you about my plans soon. I am dying to see you all. I'll send money in two or three instalments. I'll send you twenty-five thousand rupees and on receipt write that you have dispatched two large and one small photograph. Please read between the lines and confirm when you get the money. As you know, this money will be sent through unofficial channels at a higher black-market rate. I'll send three similar instalments. Deposit them in your name. The fourth instalment of twenty-five thousand should be passed on to Bhapa. That same fellow, nephew of your aunt from Jandiala, will deliver these instalments to you. Do not let anyone else know of this arrangement. I'll be paying only half the amount to the person here. The remaining half will be paid after you have received the money in India. Hence, write to me as soon as an instalment is received.

Chapter Five

Baldev's relatives, people from his village, and friends brought in a lot of presents, big and small, to be given to their folks back home. He was neither in a position to refuse anyone, nor could he carry so much weight. Most of all, he was afraid of the harassment at the hands of customs officers after arrival in Delhi. He decided to reduce some of his own things.

Sohan Singh suggested that he should stuff everything into the suitcase anyhow. He would accompany Baldev to the airport, and would bring back the excess, if any.

With a little dexterity they managed to get the luggage through, although now the prospect of facing greedy customs officers in India, and their insulting behaviour was beginning to bother Baldev Singh. However, once inside the plane he felt very happy remembering the words of his relatives who had come to see him off. 'You are very lucky to go home, Baldev Singh. You have managed this within five years of arriving here. Look at us, we are still craving for a visit,' they had said.

The air hostesses looked very charming. But he was eager for the plane to reach Delhi so that he could proceed to his village. It occurred to him that since it was the month of February, the wheat crop would be knee-high by now. He could also visualise the leaves of the sugar-cane crop yellowed by winter. The din of sugar-cane crushers and the smell of freshly made jaggery began to grip his senses.

Paramjit was carrying a basket over her head. Her face shaded by the basket was like mustard flowers blooming in the sun. He was about to clasp her in his arms when he saw his father, Jagar Singh suddenly come out of the nearby field of berseem with a sickle in his hand.

Baldev instantly dropped his outstretched arms. His right arm struck the passenger sitting beside him, and he gave Baldev a dirty look. The latter realised what had happened, and with some embarrassment apologised.

The customs fellows rummaged through each and everything. His meticulously packed things were now spread all over the floor. Mr Sharma's asinine questions had made him feel miserable. He saw C S CHAWLA written on the badge of one of the officers and proceeded towards him, thinking that a fellow Sikh would probably bail him out. But Mr Chawla turned out to be even worse. 'Why are you carrying goods for your friends? What proof do you have that these belong to your friends? Open this. What is this?' Questions kept on being bombarded at him. Petty threats and sly warnings were given to extract money. Finally, Baldev Singh decided to dump five pounds on him to get rid of this nuisance.

Ajit Singh was waiting for him outside. The brothers hugged each other and after a brief customary greeting got busy, making arrangements to make their way to the New Delhi Railway Station.

During the journey home Baldev Singh kept enquiring about each one of his family members. At times he would begin to talk about Ajit Singh's children, and then steer the conversation to Simranjit and Rashim. Actually, he wanted to know more of his wife, Paramjit. But Ajit Singh was oblivious to what Baldev was going through. True to his nature, he merely said, 'Everyone is all right. *Bibi* was unwell for a while, but now she is fine too,' and started looking out of the window of the running train.

The train gradually slowed down. When it almost came

to a crawl, Baldev spotted PHAGWARA JUNCTION written on the platform and heaved a sigh of relief. His heart started beating faster in excitement. By the time, they came out of the station, it was already getting dark.

'You stay here and watch over the luggage. I'll go and check if Jeeta is still here with his tonga,' said Ajit Singh and proceeded to the tonga halt.

Watching him standing with luggage, the rickshaw pullers came up and asked, 'Where do you want to go, *Babuji*? Come, sit.'

'No, I am not going anywhere. I am waiting for someone,' he replied each time.

Finally, Ajit Singh arrived with a tempo driver. Baldev wanted to buy some fruit for the children, but judging that Ajit Singh was impatient to reach home decided to keep quiet.

Not long after their tempo entered the village, the news travelled quickly through the lanes and by-lanes that Jagar Singh's son Baldev Singh has arrived from England.

People from the neighbouring homes came over to meet Baldev Singh. A few congratulated Jagar Singh on his son's arrival, while others rejoiced with Baldev's mother Channan Kaur. Baldev Singh himself was surrounded by excited children. His sister Mindo was overjoyed by the changed, ruddy look of her brother. Watching all this, Paramjit got so emotional that she had to go inside twice to wipe her tears. She did not want anyone to notice her tears of joy.

Once the neighbours left for their respective homes, Baldev pushed the bottle of country-made liquor aside and put the bottle of Scotch on the table. They sat chatting and drinking in the hall for a long time.

After they finished eating, noticing that it was already late in the night, Jagar Singh said, 'Baldev must be tired from his journey. All of you should retire now. Nimba, get me food for the dog and I'll also leave for the outhouse.'

Hearing this, his older daughter-in-law Preeto brought food for their dog along with a container of hot milk for Jagar Singh.

'Baldev Singh too will drink. Maybe you'll run short of milk, so do not give me any today,' said Jagar Singh, returning the container to Preeto.

'Do not worry, *Bhapaji*. There is plenty of milk. Take this,' Preeto said, declining to take back the container.

Due to exhaustion and because of having gone to bed rather late, Baldev Singh woke up pretty late. The sun was almost overhead. Those who had come to know of Baldev's arrival later, began to pour in after breakfast. Baldev's house had acquired a festive atmosphere.

During breakfast, Simranjit mentioned to her father excitedly, 'Daddyji, *Babaji* has asked you visit him at the outhouse by the well after you have eaten.'

Jagar Singh was delighted and excited by the arrival of his foreign-returned son. He wanted Baldev to visit him wearing his English suit and necktie so that the whole village could see him thereby enhancing Jagar Singh's prestige in the community.

In honour of their father's arrival from England, the children had decided to skip school. Baldev flanked by Nimba on one side and by his children on the other walked towards the outhouse. Watching them together made Jagar Singh's heart swell with pride. He took out a charpoy from inside and spread a thick sheet over it.

While they were taking a walk through their fields, Jagar Singh began to explain, 'Baldev Singh, we bought the land from the Roorkee family at an opportune time. Right up to that outer pathway, the entire wheat crop belongs to us. Just two fields in the middle belong to Ram Lal. His younger son Mohan has an embroidery unit in Phagwara. Now he has gone and joined his elder brother in Delhi. I have been eyeing these fields for quite some time. If we manage to buy these too, our holding, my son, will be the largest in the entire village.'

'How much money will be required?' asked Baldev although he did not want to.

'I am hopeful that we can close the deal within thirty-five to forty thousand rupees.'

For a moment, Baldev almost felt like telling his father to go ahead and make the deal. But then he remembered what Paramjit had told him the previous night and decided to keep quiet. He could not but agree with Paramjit. The children were growing up. Not merely growing up, very soon they would already be grown-up.

For the next ten or fifteen days he discussed everything with Paramjit without involving anyone else. Eventually, he reached the conclusion that a house was his more immediate need than buying more land. They needed to build a separate home, otherwise how would they live in just two rooms!

He gathered the courage to speak about this to his father one day, in the presence of his elder brother Ajit Singh.

'*Bhayya*, I cannot say for how long I'll be here but I think that if you agree to give me about one eighth of an acre near the pathway, I could build a house there. Then our house in the village can be used entirely by *Bhaji* and Nimba.'

'Son, I have no objection in doing that but what is worrying me is the fact that both sons of the Amritsar family have also gone abroad. They too are eyeing Ram Lal's land. So, if we could buy these two fields before building the house, that would be better,' Jagar Singh said scratching his head and making his priorities clear.

'All right. I'll consult Paramjit and the children and see what they feel about it. We'll give it a thought then...' Feeling despondent, Baldev Singh could barely manage to utter these words.

'Son, to tell you the truth one does not consult women in these matters; one consults one's brothers. And your children are too young to have any opinion. You, my boys, have become men in their own right; even then at times I have to take decisions without seeking your opinion. Think about it...'

Jagar Singh had not quite finished when Chainchal Singh from the adjoining holding came over. He immediately hugged Baldev and said, 'Look at you, Baldev Singh! It is difficult to recognise you. You almost look like a sahib now. How many years have you been away? I think at least five or six years.' He looked towards Jagar Singh.

'Yes, I think it must be five or six years now.'

The same day Nimba began pleading with Jagar Singh, 'Look *Bhapa*, had *Bhaji* really been interested in getting me to England, he would have done that by now. *Bhabi*, too, does not want him to make any efforts in this matter. She wants to leave our home as soon as possible along with *Bhaji* and the children. I am sure this idea of building a separate house is her brainchild.

'Secondly, I know that *Bhaji* has some money. Go ahead, and buy the land. That is a good idea. But if you send me to Canada through that agent who has managed to dispatch Surain Singh's son Meeka there, I promise I'll buy you the land within a year. That is my promise. I'll be earning there. I have neither wife nor children. So, I'll send all of my earnings to you. And come and get married whenever you'll ask me to.'

Plans of building a separate house were relegated to a later day and the focus shifted to arranging for Nimba's passage to Canada. Baldev Singh did not want to annoy his father. His mother, Channan Kaur also pleaded day and night on Nimba's behalf. Eventually, Jagar Singh contributed half the money required, took the rest from Baldev Singh, and Nimba was sent off to Canada. After about two months, the news of his having reached Canada arrived and the entire household was overcome with joy. Jagar Singh and Ajit Singh gladly accepted Baldev's plan to build a separate house near the pathway, if he so wished.

Baldev Singh began to build his house with a lot of enthusiasm. What a joy it was for them – one's own house!

So many dreams and delights of one's life are associated with the house. A woman's attachment to her house is even deeper.

At times there would be scarcity of cement; at other times something else would impede the progress. Even then, after four months the walls had been raised, the lintel placed and the doors and windows made. But due to non-availability of cement, the finishing was still pending. Flooring, too, was lying incomplete.

While Baldev Singh was busy trying to complete the house, preparation for Mindo's wedding began. The groom was on a visit from England. Channan Kaur, once again, began pleading to Baldev Singh, 'Look, son! You know how much your Ajit *Bhaji* earns. There are other expenses of the family too. Even then he is ready to pitch in whatever he can. Whatever money your *bhapa* had saved has been almost spent on sending Nimba abroad. If there is anything left, he too, will contribute. But we expect the maximum from you. This alliance is too good to be missed. Moreover, your sister will go to England if she marries this boy. It will be good for both of you to have each other in a foreign land. This alliance…'

The construction of the house halted at whatever stage it was. In one of the rooms, instead of the intended terrazzo flooring, ordinary flooring was laid.

The arrangements for Mindo's wedding began. Baldev Singh and his family shifted to the new house, in whatever stage of completion it was.

Mindo was married off with abundant pomp and pageantry.

Once the rabi crop was sold and some money came into their hands, Baldev Singh began to think of completing the flooring and painting of their house. Cement was available, yet not available. The entire stock would disappear from the back doors of the godowns. He would barely manage to get a bag or two from time to time. Who could he complain to? He had to buy some of his requirement, from the black market. That too, through recommendations of people who mattered.

One day he managed to get two bags from Jandiala and one from Nurmahal.

Concrete houses would get very hot in the months of June and July and would continue to radiate heat from their walls right up to midnight. Baldev had already completed the wiring of the house, but was running from pillar to post to get the electricity connection. Exhausted, he reached home one evening, washed and sat down on the rooftop fanning himself with a hand-held fan. The air was solidly still.

His children, chasing a ball in the courtyard, were sweating profusely. Paramjit was washing clothes. He felt like taking a walk through their fields. That is when he spotted his older brother Ajit Singh approaching. A wave of excitement ran through him. '*Bhaji* is coming here. Ask Simran to go and get some ice and soda from the shop,' he excitedly informed Paramjit who was washing clothes sitting by their courtyard tap.

But Ajit Singh went straight ahead into the alley leading to their house inside the village. He did not even notice his younger brother looking at him, from the rooftop. Sadness overcame Baldev. He felt empty in spite of everything and everyone around him. A man, alone and insecure, helpless and exposed. He tried to look for the reasons for his despondency.

Then he shouted for Simran who came running to him.

'Son, I have a slight uneasiness in my stomach. Maybe I have eaten something that didn't suit me. Tell your mother that there is a bottle lying in the box containing quilts. Get that from her and bring it over. Also get some ice and a bottle of soda. The rest of the soda you may drink.'

After finishing his second peg, he pushed the glass away. He felt as if he had tracked the reason for his sadness.

Dreams! They enthuse and stimulate. These are the wings on which daily life soars above its drudgery. One must not let the dreams die. Whether they come true or not, is another matter altogether. And if dreams were woven around an attainable desire, why would they not come true! Life without dreams is no life. It is a colourless life – completely bland.

For a long time, similar thoughts kept crossing his mind.

After dinner, Paramjit informed him that she had heard that one of the political parties was going to stage a play in the village community hall to garner votes.

'Which party? The Congress or the Communists?'

'I don't know.'

'Anyway, whichever party it is. Some consider Congress as their own party and the others are close to the Communist Party. Their flags are made of the same cloth. Isn't that so?' His voice was faltering. Then he spoke again. 'All right. Let us go and watch the play.'

'But you have had a lot of drink today. If you are going to create a scene there, it would be better to stay at home. We'll go only if you promise that you'll sit quietly.'

'I have created enough scenes in my college days. I am not going to create any more.'

That night, instead of his customary trousers, he wore a *chadra* like others and tied his turban, too, in the local manner, with one end left hanging.

Some people were sitting on a dhurrie; he went up and stood behind them. Simran, Rashim and Daljit sat on the dhurrie in front. Paramjit went and sat on the dhurrie spread in the veranda for the womenfolk.

In the beginning, a man came up to the microphone and said, 'It maybe any party, but if it does not empathise with the people of India, it does not deserve their votes…'

'Empathy with the people or with votes?' someone from the back interrupted the speaker.

The speaker began again, 'There can be no India without its people. India exists because of its people. The people are the pride of India…'

A chorus rang out from the stage, 'In the entire world, India is the best…'

Again a loud voice boomed from the back, 'In the entire world, the most corrupt is…'

When everybody started staring at Baldev Singh, he suddenly realised that perhaps he had uttered something inappropriate. Many of the spectators thought that probably the *Jutt* had too much to drink that night.

Once money saved in England dissipated, they began to face economic adversity. When he could not find any suitable job openings in India, Baldev Singh was left with no other option except to knock at the doors of England once again.

One day Rashim came home and told him that her teacher Parveen Sharma wanted to meet him. She had earlier visited their home to meet him, but now she had asked him to come and meet her in the school.

He was reminded of his college days. Along with these thoughts, memories of some other events came rushing back. He remembered the days spent with Rama Sahani, when they were in love. She had just begun to teach in Phagwara. They had already known each other for more than a year when Baldev told her, 'Rama, I do not want to tear myself away from you but I am compelled to. I am preparing to leave for England in search of a better future. I would like you to get married while I am still here.'

'Balli, even though I know that you are married and have children I have loved you. I have not loved you to break someone's family or to take away what is rightfully hers. I have loved you for the sake of love, and still love you. Just continue to bestow on me the love that is my share. I do not need to get married.'

In England, Baldev would remember Rama's words almost everyday. For quite some time they kept writing to each other directly or indirectly. Rama had also applied for a voucher, but the list was so long that her turn did not come. Later, Baldev sponsored her for a short visit, too. Meanwhile, her family had persuaded her to marry a lawyer from Jalandhar.

When Baldev met Rama after returning to India, he could not see any trace of their earlier love in her eyes. Her love was now confined to her children and her husband's home. How long could she have kept her love for Baldev alive, in her heart or in her eyes! She was no longer the same Rama Sahani. After getting married she had turned into Rama Bhasin.

From Rama, his thoughts drifted back to Parveen Sharma. It occurred to him that these were mere mirages of love like the mirages of water in deserts, making a man wander here and there. Maybe this was one of the reasons that he never felt settled in England; always hankering to get back to the village. Otherwise, why couldn't a man settle in the place where he works! In times to come, commercial cooperation between countries would become imperative for their mutual progress and then the entire world would feel like one's own.

Often one's own country doesn't treat its citizens as her own. The insulting behaviour begins at the main portal – the airport – itself. One's country is made up of one's own people, but now our people have lost their warmth and affability for fellow countrymen. Relationships are based on material considerations.

Chapter Six

Before returning to England, Baldev decided to unburden himself by writing a letter to his friend Sohan Singh from his village.

20 September 1971

Dear Sohan Singh,

I hope that you are well. All the dreams that I had carried with me to India have slowly dissipated. I had thought that I'd be able to find a job or start some work in India and that it would be possible to enjoy the warmth of one's family by living here. But the people here, in the village, are not innocent and simple like they were in the earlier days. Their heartstrings are tugged less by emotional cords and more by material gains. Once the television reaches homes in India, like it has in England, the traditional hospitality will disappear completely. Even blood ties will retain some meaning for only for a few.

The other problem is that jobs are auctioned here. Nothing is possible without a bribe. Whether you want a copy of the land record from the patwari, or you need to book a seat on a train; whether you want to procure cement, or you wish to buy fertiliser – no one will lend you a ear until and unless you offer a bribe.

For the leaders, people are not people but mere voters. Be it Darbara Singh, or be it Harkishen Singh Surjit; no one is concerned with the travails of the people. Even the conductors here think in terms of 'passengers' not 'people'; and that is true about private as well as government-owned transport. In

England even the conductors are so polite, always saying 'thank you' to everyone. Hence I have decided to come back to England.

If possible, please find an opening for me in the Ford factory. What are the rates of the houses there? I'll have to buy a small house and get my wife and children over. Initially, I may have to live with you, bag and baggage.

I'll write to you again once my seat is confirmed. As it is, there is just one month left before I complete two years here.

More later,

Yours,

Baldev

While they were eating dinner, Paramjit told Baldev that she had met *Bapu's* friend Niranjan Singh in the village. 'The same Niranjan Singh who gets his pension from England and lives here now. He was saying that you may stay with his sons till such time you get a job. His sons may even help in getting you a job. I have forgotten the name of the city they live in, but he mentioned that it is close to the airport.'

Baldev was much relieved to hear this. One never knows who one may need while living in a foreign land. He must get their phone numbers and addresses tomorrow. Baldev made a mental note.

In the morning, immediately after breakfast, Baldev picked up his bicycle and set off for Samravan to meet Niranjan Singh.

Niranjan Singh was reading the newspaper sitting under a tree in his haveli located on the peripheral road. Baldev Singh greeted him respectfully and enquired after his health out of politeness.

'Well, my health, my son, is as it usually is in old age. Some part of the body or other keeps on giving trouble.'

'But, *Tayaji* you are in much better health than the others of your age. You look younger by almost ten or twelve years,' Baldev said to please him.

'By the grace of *Wahe Guru*, I have never seen bad days. I've always had enough to eat and live well. Had I not gone to England, maybe I would have been dead by now. Remember Gyana, the wrestler? What a hefty man he was! But poverty crushed him, and he died in such dire circumstances. Of course, you know all that. May God never put anyone through the grind of poverty. At a time such as this, forget about relatives, even your own family members desert you.'

Meanwhile, Niranjan Singh's helper brought tea and they kept talking, while drinking tea. At last, he picked up his son's letter from the shelf, showed it to Baldev Singh and said, 'Write down the address carefully. As you may know, Southall is right next to the airport. Write down the phone number, too. I'll give that to you in a minute. One of them will come and receive you. Bheera, in fact, works at the airport. Do not worry about anything. Until you get a job, treat it as your own home. Stay with them as one of their own kin. They will also try and get you a job somewhere. If our people do not help each other in a foreign country, who will?'

'*Tayaji*, when do you plan to visit England?' Baldev enquired for the sake of it.

'I have worked enough. Why should I go to England now? Although there is a gurdwara and a park for walks nearby, I wish to spend the few years of my old age here. If one is healthy, even this age is not bad. I must say, your *tayee* takes good care of me. I am happy with my children, too. My pension is also more than enough for my needs.

'You know that uncle of yours from the cantonment? He buys rum, cheap from the army canteen and brings it over for me. I always have five or seven bottles in reserve. If one wishes, even this age can be enjoyed like the younger days. In youth, one is obliged to follow a schedule. At this age, you do not have to follow any schedule. For example, you may go to sleep, whenever you wish and get up whenever you want. There is no pressure of any kind.

'The responsibilities of raising a family deny one the freedom of this kind in the younger days. Of course, one is no longer that fit physically, but who wants to do weights at this age? Oh yes, there is one more deficiency. But nowadays I am not much bothered by that because your *tayee* is not going to run away at this age.'

Having said this, *Taya* began to laugh loudly. Then he pressed Baldev's elbow with one of his hands and said, 'Go and tell them that they should not worry about the old man. As long as my woman is there, I will not wear down, and probably won't even die. But if she dies before me, it won't be easy for me to go on living.'

This thought made Niranjan Singh a little serious indeed.

Chapter Seven

Baldev had been living in Southall for five months already. Initially he did not like the job of a bus conductor. But with the continuous arrival of new families from Punjab in England, there were opportunities to flirt with Punjabi lasses, adding some romance to his life. With the passage of time, his eyes would focus on certain faces or seek them out at particular times.

Sometimes he would yearn to meet his old friends Ravinder, Cheema, Sohan and Gulati, but as he was working all seven days, there was no time at all for such activities.

During one weekend, Sohan Singh came over. That night Baldev spoke at length about the two faces that he would often encounter on the bus. While leaving, Sohan Singh just mentioned in a cautionary tone, 'There is no harm in flirting a bit. But this emotional attachment should remain within limits. You have left your wife and children behind who are dependent on you. Try to save money as soon as you can, buy a house and call them. There is the question of your children's future and besides, two of you will be earning once Paramjit arrives.'

Time like seasons moves on at its usual pace. Time is not bothered whether anyone keeps in step with it or not. Baldev spent many more months working as a bus conductor.

Sohan's calls would make Baldev happy, but at the same time sad, too, as he was no longer in touch with those faces.

The Ford company had begun to hire workers. Sohan

reminded Baldev to fill the forms. Soon after his medical check-up, Baldev received the appointment letter.

Baldev had rented a room in Sohan's house. He had a well-paid clean job. Besides the meagre amount that he send home to cover his family's expenses, Baldev concentrated on saving the rest for a deposit for the house.

Within a year he managed to save enough to buy a house. The dream of buying a house and getting his family to England was in his subconscious mind all the time.

A man called Daulati, around fifty years of age, worked with him. He belonged to Ambala. Their acquaintance soon turned into friendship.

When Baldev told Daulati his objective of buying a house and inviting his family, Daulati said immediately, 'Look, I consider you as my younger brother. Just two houses away from my house, I have seen a board saying FOR SALE. If you want to buy a house, buy that house. You will not get a better location. There is a school nearby and the bus stop right opposite to it. It is a mere fifteen-minute walk from our workplace; you won't have to travel either by car or by bus. I'll get your wife a job in the food factory. Tell me, what else would you be requiring?'

Daulati fixed an appointment for 2 p.m. the following Saturday, and soon after the shift got over, he took Baldev to inspect the house.

When Baldev and Sohan Singh looked over the house, Daulati pointed out many of its positive and not-so-positive features and convinced Baldev to buy the house in Ilford.

Buying the house in Ilford, further cemented Baldev's relationship with Daulati's family. He had indeed become Daulati's younger brother, and his wife, Sarla, became his sister-in-law.

Each time he took a step in the direction of Daulati's house, a few forbidden fantasies also accompanied him.

Sarla was about thirty-five years old. Daulati was above

fifty. Daulati had many lodgers in his house. He would always rent out rooms either to elderly men or to married people. Daulati knew that although Baldev was still single, his family would be joining him soon.

Often Daulati would behave as if he was oblivious of what was going on. He would merely say, 'Look, you are my brother. She is your sister-in-law. She takes as much care of you as she takes of me.'

There are many relationships in this world that have no convictions behind them. They are meaningless, created merely for social niceties, so that one does not transgress the accepted social norms. But every brother cannot be a 'Lakshman', nor can every sister-in-law be 'Sita'. Moreover, those two had belonged to a different epoch.

In history, as well as in mythology there are many instances of even gods and sages succumbing to temptation. Baldev and Sarla, after all, were mere mortals.

Sarla's being was like a river flowing next to him and its allure mesmerised Baldev. His thoughts were like a ripened field, which swayed in the breeze that emanated from Sarla. She had done BA in music from Saraswati Music School, and Baldev was a lover of art.

When Baldev dispatched the sponsorship documents for his family, Daulati decided to celebrate the event by inviting Sohan Singh and Baldev to his home for dinner on a weekend.

They went to the pub near Daulati's house while Sarla got busy preparing the meal. Daulati had gone to the toilet, when Sohan asked, 'What is the matter, my friend? Uncle is looking a bit off colour today.'

'If you call your elder brother "Uncle", then Sarla will become your aunt,' Baldev, too, replied in the same vein. He knew that Sohan was aware of all their secrets. There was no need to hide anything from Sohan Singh. He could not have hidden anything from such a close friend.

'But I want to know why Daulati is not happy? In fact, Sarla should be feeling sad and not Daulati.'

They saw Daulati returning from the toilet and quickly changed the subject. All of them had three glasses of beer each and came back to Daulati's house.

Once there, they opened a bottle of whisky. They were sitting in the lounge and Daulati said, 'Go, Baldev and get some ice and soda from the fridge. Also ask you sister-in-law if the chicken is ready. If it is, ask her to send some to us in a bowl.'

Daulati put on a ghazal recorded in Sarla's voice: 'Love has no reason, no justification.'

Listening to her dulcet voice, Sohan felt that Sarla was like an incense stick, spreading fragrance all the way from Daulati's house to Baldev's home.

Daulati knew that Sohan Singh was aware of everything and that he was an upright and principled person. He was not the kind who would make fun of his friends; in fact, he would stand by them always.

After consuming two pegs Daulati was already tipsy. His speech was slurred. Addressing Sohan Singh he said, 'You know Sohan Singh, we have gathered here today to celebrate the imminent arrival of our younger sister-in-law. I really wish that our wives would get along the same way as we have been. Only then can life be wonderful. What do you say, Sohan Singh? You are an intelligent man.' Having said this he started looking at Sohan Singh expectantly, as if awaiting his endorsement.

Sohan Singh understood the import of these words fully, but decided to keep quiet. He merely said, 'Yes, it should be like that.'

Then he looked at Baldev meaningfully. Baldev smiled discreetly and looked at the picture on the wall. The colours appeared to be, burnished and then faded. Then the images became blurred and he began to see double. He was inebriated.

Their conversation was light and jovial over the drinks. Looking at Daulati, Baldev said, 'Looks like elder brother is tipsy today. I think, I'd better go and ask Sarla to get the food.' Having said this he went to the kitchen. The children were busy watching television in the drawing room.

Sarla began to lay the table. Baldev brought the bowl of vegetables. Sohan felt as if Daulati had passed on the matchstick in his hand to Baldev to light the incense stick...

There was something in Daulati's mind that he wanted to express to Sohan Singh. Addressing him, haltingly, he said, 'Sohan Singh, you are not a stranger to me. A man can share his joys and sorrows only with his friends... You see, the matter is... It is like someone going to the market. But if you do not have a penny in your pocket, how can you think of shopping? A man must have money. Whether he spends it or not is a different matter altogether. Similarly, if you have the treasure of strength, you feel secure. You can use it whenever you wish to. But if you have nothing with you, how can you think of living and enjoying life? Are you following me? You know, since I was injured in the factory... in a bad way... since that time...'

His faltering words laid bare some deeper wounds.

'Do not worry, elder brother. Your friendship will continue the way it is. If any problem arises, we'll solve that together. I am there for you. No one can dare to create any misunderstanding. No one is at fault here. We are friends and will remain friends through the years. Our children will sow the seeds of our friendship in the next generation.'
Meanwhile, Baldev and Sarla had brought food to the coffee table in the lounge and they chatted while they ate.

The incense stick spread its intoxicating fragrance all around. The house always had a pleasant atmosphere.

Chapter Eight

As soon as Baldev received the key to the house in Ilford he dispatched tickets for his family to come to England.

Over the weekend, Sohan Singh and Daulati helped Baldev to paint and wallpaper the house. Within five or six weeks they decorated the house and brought in some furniture. Although the furniture was bought second-hand, all the rooms looked spruced up, as the previous owner had left his curtains and carpets behind.

Since the day Sohan Singh had bought a new car, he had been persuading Baldev Singh to take driving lessons. Daulati had said, 'When we were new here, everyone used to say that there was no need to buy a car. But I think those people were idiots. They did not realise how convenient it is to possess a car. Rain or storm, day or night, one can step out whenever one wishes. Otherwise, one freezes standing and waiting at bus stops. Besides, we were single in those days. Four beds in one room, and seven or eight people to share that room. Nowadays, people don't even want to keep lodgers because they feel that keeping outsiders in the home is no better than living in a rented accommodation. I agree with Sohan Singh that you should take driving lessons. By the time your family arrives, you would have passed the test and then you may buy a car for about five to seven hundred pounds.'

Their argument convinced Baldev and he started taking driving lessons twice a week. Once he had mastered the basics, Sohan Singh began to take him on practice drives in his car every Sunday, with a learner's L sign displayed on it. Thanks to the encouragement given by his friends, and due to his own hard work and perseverance, Baldev Singh passed the driving test and bought an old Cortina. Of course, he did not clear the test at one go, but succeeded in his third attempt.

He began giving a lift to three fellows who worked with him at the Ford factory. His petrol bills were taken care of through this arrangement. At times, he could not help thinking that it would have been much better had he learnt driving immediately after arriving in England. He would have managed to complete his evening course in Eastham College and would have become an engineer like Atwal. But then, one cannot bring back the time that is already gone, and as such should not fret over it.

The trees were resplendent with new leaves. Blooming flowers indicated the height of spring. May in India is a month of raging heat, but in England it is just the beginning of summer. But this year, due to sleet, it was still necessary to use an overcoat; otherwise the neck would turn stiff with cold.

Although Baldev had advised them to carry warm clothes along with them in the plane, Paramjit had ignored his advice going by the heat wave in India, and had put all of them in a suitcase. When they arrived at Heathrow, the children were in half-sleeved shirts and Paramjit was wrapped in a light shawl.

Their teeth began to chatter as soon as they came out of the airport building. Baldev hurriedly passed on the luggage to Sohan Singh and ran along with his children and Paramjit to his parked car. He switched on the heater and it warmed the car within a few minutes.

Before leaving the airport, Baldev looked at Paramjit sitting beside him and at his children on the rear seat, and asked, 'Anyone wants to go for a pee?'

'No,' one of them replied from the rear seat.

Baldev started following Sohan Singh's car.

'Is this our car?' asked Paramjit.

'Yes, our car. Belongs to all of us,' Baldev said swiftly.

'But you never told us that you had already bought a car.'

'I bought it just two weeks ago. There was no time to tell you. The thought of how I would take you home with so much luggage and how we would manage without a car bothered me. Didn't I tell you to wear warm clothes for your travel?'

'But it was scorching in Punjab. We thought that by now it would be summer here, too.' Paramjit looked back at the children as if seeking their affirmation.

They were travelling towards London and the children gaped at the colourful neon signs, mesmerised by the sights and sounds of this new world.

'Daddy, how far is our house from here?' asked Simran who was twelve or thirteen years old.

'About twenty minutes more and we shall be home,' Baldev replied sharing their excitement.

'Is there anyone at home or is it locked?' asked Simran.

'We left your auntie Sarla at home. We thought you'd be hungry and she could prepare some food for you in the meanwhile. Remember that uncle with a cap, Daulati, who was with Sohan Singh? Sarla is his wife. You see that car, which is three cars ahead of us, with a suitcase tied on the top rack? They are in that car.'

As soon as they reached home, Daulati and Sohan Singh stacked their bags in the front room and the hall. The gas heater in the front room was on and had made the room quite warm. The intense cold they experienced on stepping out of the car, went away the moment they entered the main room.

They had barely sat down when Sarla brought hot tea and pakoras for them. She had already kneaded the flour and made a vegetable, and a meat dish. After the customary introductions, it did not take them long to get comfortable with each other.

To celebrate the arrival of Baldev's family, they decided to visit the King's Head pub for a couple of glasses of beer, before opening the whisky bottle at home.

After the men left for the pub, Sarla showed Paramjit and the children around their house. She explained everything to them – how to use the toilet seat, how to switch on the gas cooker and the heater.

By about nine o'clock the bottle of whisky was opened, and a bowl of meat was served on the table. In a spirited vein, Baldev pushed a small glass towards Simran and said, 'Here, my lad! It will drive the cold from your bones. You were shivering like a lamb at the airport. Eat the meat and relish your auntie's cooking.' Having said that, he looked towards Sarla and smiled faintly.

After the children had eaten a plateful of meat each, Baldev said, 'Eat to your heart's fill. There is plenty of meat cooked. In India we used to buy a kilo of meat once in a blue moon. Then add a kilo of potatoes and four jugs full of water into it. We would also add a fistful of red chillies, so that no one could eat much. We would barely get one piece per person and yet after eating that meagre ration everyone would belch and say "we have eaten meat today".'

'It is good that you left India. Otherwise you would have been fighting hunger there,' said Sohan Singh.

'Very true,' Daulati endorsed what Sohan Singh said.

The next day was Sunday and the day following that was the Spring bank holiday. Hence they would not have to get up early the next morning. The children and both the women ate first. Meanwhile, the men finished their first bottle and looked forward to opening another one. The children watched television while Sarla and Paramjit got to know each other better.

At about midnight Sohan Singh and Daulati Ram left for

their respective homes.

Before retiring, Baldev told everyone that the following two days were holidays. 'People sleep late and get up late. Everyone can sleep to one's heart's content. They can have baths in the morning. People in this country do not bathe more than twice a week. There is no need to bathe daily. One does not sweat here or get dirty. Only those people bathe daily who work in a heavily polluted environment. Such workers have bathing arrangements in their factories. They clean themselves at their workplace before coming home. Some people spend less time at home and more in the pubs. Midland has many foundries where the work is dirty. Mostly people from the *Jutt* community, who had been engaged in wheat cutting and thrashing in India, take up such jobs. Mindo's husband used to work in a foundry. Once I went to see him. To tell you the truth, I could not even recognise him – arms padded with sacks, his head covered with ash. It is true that they earn more, but they spend that much more on drinking beer. If you want to visit these people, you'll be able to find them only inside a pub.'

Baldev, in an inebriated state, was spinning ceaselessly.

In a few days, Paramjit and the children became familiar with their surroundings. Soon they came to know all the shops and businesses like where to buy groceries and where to do their laundry. The children's schools were also nearby. Rashim and Daljit's school was close to the house; Simran's was about half a mile away. They were admitted into these schools according to their age.

The younger two made friends with the other children very quickly and within a year learnt enough English to get by. But Simran, who had to join much older children, remained bashful for long, and took time to make friends.

The white children would taunt them sometimes, giving the children an inferiority complex. At times they would tell their parents about such incidents, at other times they would keep it to themselves.

Deepo, wife of Pal Singh Sanghera of Bilga village and Baldev's wife Paramjit worked in the same factory. At that time, Pal Singh lived in Canning Town. Both women shared the same wavelength. Their visits to each other's homes gradually, paved the way for friendship between their families.

Not just Deepo and Paramjit, Pal Singh and Baldev Singh also became good friends. The same was true of their children.

One day Pal Singh Sanghera called up, 'Baldev Singh, what is being cooked for dinner?'

'Today, my friend, just masoor lentils,' Baldev Singh replied.

'In that case, all of you come over to our home. We have cooked mutton and chicken today.' Pal Singh immediately extended an invitation.

'But my friend, one should sometimes eat masoor lentils too. Had we stayed in India, this is what we would be eating all the time.'

'True, very true. In India we would have been eating lentils. But we are not in India now, are we? We are in England. Isn't that so? Come over to our place today. We'll go over to yours some other day. In any case, we do not have to get into this petty accounting. My home is yours too. Please reach by five o'clock. Besides, today another *Jutt*, Jimmy Carter, has become the president. The whole world has to forcibly celebrate the election of a US president. Moreover, we have one more reason to celebrate.'

'What is that?' Baldev's voice was full of curiosity.

'You see, near our house, on Court Road a gurdwara has been set up. Although it is an old building, it is very spacious. We'll go there for a short while.'

'After the death of Blair Peach in Southall, the racial

tension in your area seems to be on the rise. Just yesterday the Anti-Nazi League and National Front supporters clashed violently. One is afraid of even going to a pub. Come over to our side today. We know the guv'nor of King's Road pub. The atmosphere too, is good there. We'll go to the gurdwara some other day.'

'What you are saying is true. Today, too, there was a lot of disturbance because of the demonstration held by the Nazi and Socialist parties. We are going to a pub to relax for a few hours, to drink a couple of glasses. What is the use of going somewhere and getting bashed up? Okay, let us do it this way. I know that you have everything in your home, but I'll put the chicken dish and a bottle of country-made liquor in my boot. This bottle is of a very good quality – entirely made of oranges and grapes.'

When everything progresses smoothly, one does not notice the passing years. Life carried on...

No one noticed that nine years had gone by. Simranjit's marriage was fixed with Pal Singh Sanghera's daughter Kiranjit, but they were thinking of getting a groom for Rashim from India. Daljit was still busy finishing his course in electronics.

With the increase in the demand for space, they were beginning to find their first house inadequate. Baldev Singh thought of selling the house and buying a new four-bedroom one.

Deepo advised Baldev, '*Bhaji*, do not sell this house. The amount you will spend on paying the agents and lawyers can easily pay for the repairs of another house. What difference is it going to make if you have one extra bedroom? After you beget grandsons, even that house will seem small. You keep this house and buy that corner house, the one on sale. Find out about that house. That house needs repairs; its outer windows are almost in shreds. It is possible that you may get it cheap. And what are we relatives for? To whatever extent possible, we'll help you. We'll repair that house jointly.'

Baldev found Deepo's advice sensible. Though he did not say it in so many words, he observed how wise she was.

Once home, Pal Singh said to his wife, 'It is their internal matter, whether they wish to sell the house or keep it. Have they ever interfered in your matters? Why must you give unsolicited advice?'

'*Jatta*, these things are beyond you. Who knows if our Kiran will be happy in their joint family? If they buy another house, Simranjit and Kiran can stay in the old house and the older couple along with Daljit could shift to the new house. Rashim is not going to stay there for long; she'll be married soon. They will stay separately, and yet nearby. That is almost like staying together. In fact, you, too, should give them the same advice.'

'Amazing! Our *Jatti* has become shrewd after coming to England. In India, you would not have progressed beyond the chores of cutting crops,' said Pal Singh in jest.

Baldev arranged a meeting between his sister, Mindo and the prospective bride. After her approval, the date for Simranjit's wedding was fixed. The invitation cards were dispatched to India and Canada also.

Channan Kaur and Jagar Singh were especially requested to come and attend their grandson's wedding. Mindo, too, implored her mother to attend the wedding.

However, Jagar Singh suggested to Baldev that instead of him, he should sponsor and send tickets for his elder brother Ajit Singh and his elder son Bikkar Singh.

On reaching Heathrow, they were allowed a three-month stay. Everybody was very happy that Ajit Singh and his son had come to partake in the marriage festivities.

It was a very simple wedding. The *Anand Karaj* was solemnised at the Court Road gurdwara and after that there were arrangements made for a community meal at the nearby marriage hall.

At one of the tables, some guests were sipping beer and talking to each other. 'Good that they did not call all and sundry to make a show. Otherwise people have the habit of distributing invitations indiscriminately…'

Someone else from the adjoining table said, 'I have heard that initially the boy and the girl were keen on booking a large hall in London. Then Baldev Singh explained to them that only those who have no mind of their own imitate others, and that one should conduct oneself in such a manner that others feel like emulating.'

'But only a wise man would emulate something wise. Most of our people behave like mindless sheep instead,' the man sitting opposite expressed his opinion.

One night, Paramjit shared her thoughts with Baldev. 'I think *Bhaji* is probably satisfied with the simple wedding ceremonies. But what I have gathered from Bikkar's utterances, is that *Bahenji*, Preeto and *Bibiji* were expecting to be presented with some ornaments. Let us get rings of ten to fifteen grams each made for *Bibi*, *Bhapa* and Bikkar. For *Bhaji* we can get a bracelet made of about forty grams of gold. For the rest, in any case we'll be buying clothes and material. We must do this to please our relatives.'

'Look, I leave all these womanly matters to you. Do whatever you think is right. Just let me know how much money you require. After all, we save money for such occasions only. If this gesture is going to give pleasure to our parents and siblings, then it is not a bad deal at all. But take Mindo's advice, too. Find out what she has to say.'

'Oh, yes! We must buy rings for Mindo and Charan also. Mindo may not say anything but Charan is not going to let it go. He'll certainly remonstrate some day.'

'All right. Buy whatever is necessary for them, too,' said Baldev, resignedly.

As Ajit Singh had wanted, their return flight for India was booked two months from then.

When they left, each of their suitcases weighted twenty-five kilos and hand baggages seven kilos. The entire family had come to see them off at the airport.

Baldev Singh and his family wanted them to stay longer so that they could take them around England for a vacation, and even to some nice places outside England. As it happens, whenever people visit from one's native land, one is full of affection and reverence for them.

Chapter Nine

It was the eighteenth birthday of Sohan Singh's elder son Kuldip. On his wife's insistence, Sohan Singh had booked a small hall, although he used to ridicule such celebrations. But faced with an absolutely adamant wife, he decided not to give in.

The hall was chock-a-block with people. The numbers of people were more than the seats available. It looked as if Sohan Singh's wife had distributed invitation cards to all her colleagues working with her in the pickle factory.

Snacks were being served and someone was devouring pakoras in a corner; another was eating samosas with chutney. There were some white folks, too, enjoying the Indian delicacies. One white man was eating a samosa with some difficulty. Perhaps it was too hot for his palate.

When conviviality, induced by beer and whisky, began to make itself felt, the noise level also increased. Indian music blared making more noise than music. But for the second and third generation Indians, this was the real stuff. They were enjoying jumping around on some broken seats, their movements resembling those of the bhangra.

When some boys proceeded towards the stage to dance the bhangra, Cheema, Sanghera, Daulati and Sohan Singh saw the seats vacated and quickly occupied them. They could hardly hear themselves above the noise.

When the aggressive beat of music combined with the heady effects of liquor would begin to grip some, they would go ahead and join the group dancing the bhangra.

Watching this, two young white girls also took to the floor. Following them, their white partners, too, began to dance. Later, when those white men left their companions on stage to tuck into the hot succulent chicken pieces, the Indian men took the opportunity and went ahead; ostensibly to dance with the girls, but actually to ogle at their sculpted bodies with greedy eyes, while indulging in some half-baked dance steps. They craved for their touch. Poor men!

Slowly, a number of Punjabi girls and women joined in and the stage became crowded. Those who had been standing until then managed to grab seats by the tables. Gajjan Basi and Ravinder had been sitting with their backs to the stage. But as soon as the opportunity came, they changed seats and moved to a place facing the stage.

Joginder Singh Kailay, who had been talking to Tony for a long time, came and sat next to Baldev Singh. Tony shook hands with Sohan Singh and congratulated him on his son's eighteenth birthday, and praised the Indian food and their hospitality.

Mindful of the fact that Tony was surrounded by conversation going on in Punjabi, Joginder would say a few words to him in English, from time to time.

Someone mentioned Punjab and Ravinder immediately asked, 'Kailay Sahib! You had bought a plot in Jalandhar, in Adarsh Nagar. What have you done with that?'

'What could I have done? I think when I go to India next, I'll give the responsibility to my brother-in-law in Shahkot. I'll get the plans approved and begin the construction. After that, the construction can go on slowly. But I want the work to begin while I am there. Some unskilled masons screwed up the project in the beginning itself. These days anyone can claim to be a building contractor. They do not do or know anything, but hire cheap *bhayya* labour to execute the job.

'The other problem is my sons. They say that since we are not going back to India why must we waste money on building a house there? Who is there waiting for us? But I keep thinking that when we were displaced from Pakistan, we moved to Delhi. By the time we were beginning to feel settled in India, we left for Uganda. In Uganda, we thought this was where we were going to live and eventually die. We had forgotten Delhi, and never even dreamt that we would have to leave Uganda for London, one day. So, the fear of being displaced haunts me. If we had to move tomorrow, what would we do? If we have a house in our own country, we'd at least have a place to go to. To tell you the truth, I have spent all my life settling down only to be displaced. My elder brother and sister were killed while crossing over from Pakistan...' he could not hold back his tears.

After a while, when Joginder Singh had composed himself, Sohan Singh said, 'Kailay Sahib, this fear in your mind is uncalled for. The English are not heartless. They are an intelligent race. They are not like us to get swayed by the propaganda of political parties and indulge in arson or turn into religious fanatics, in the name of religion. All this talk about racism is a gimmick, raked up by a few vile men. Nobody is going to throw us out of this country.'

'What should we do, my friend? Kailay Sahib's children are objecting to his constructing a house, but our children have been pestering us to demolish the old house in the village and construct a bungalow instead, like Bheera has made.'

'You stay put here. How often are you going to visit India? I can see you living there! First you'll squander your hard-earned money and then begin to think about what to do with the constructed house – whether to sell or to keep it. If you build in a city, there is still a possibility of making some money. But anything constructed in a village will not even get back half its cost. Of course, if you wish to be generous towards your brother and nephews then it is all right. They may or may not praise your munificence but at least they'll live in style, thanks to you,' Sohan Singh said in a sarcastic manner.

'Who has the time to praise anyone's generosity? But yes, they'll certainly live there happily and that too with airs,' Ravinder could not resist adding his bit.

As soon as the music stopped, food was served on trays. People put them on the tables, wherever there was space available. Others used any handy surface as a makeshift table.

Mr Gulati and his family, who had been sitting in a far corner until then, brought their food trays and joined Sohan Singh and others at their table. People were gathered in small groups, each discussing their own particular interests. Everyone was speaking in a voice louder than usual. Taking a bite, Gulati Sahib said, 'Quite a lot of what you are talking about is beyond my understanding. You village folk do not speak proper Punjabi.'

'No, Mr Gulati. Your accusation is totally incorrect. Whatever we, the village folk, speak is in fact the proper Punjabi. When we had arrived here, we used to accuse the whites of not speaking proper English, because we did not know what correct English was. Now we have realised that, in fact what the whites speak is correct English. We may not know it that way, but may learn it from our children.' Ravinder gave Mr Gulati an extended lecture.

'One more thing – those of us who have been in close contact with the whites, have learnt English. That is why I do not agree with you when you say that we, the village people do not know Punjabi. We not only speak Punjabi, we also live and breathe it.'

Some women had begun to gather the empty trays in black plastic bags. Almost everyone had finished eating. By and by, people started to get into their cars, while a few debated whether to call for a minicab. Others walked to the bus stop. Still others were on the lookout for a possible lift. The party that had started at 6 p.m. had ended by 11 p.m.

Chapter Ten

The decision to get a groom for Rashim from India was finalised through Ajit Singh's letter. To save money, it was felt that the groom's photograph was sufficient to come to a decision and he should be sponsored. However, Ravinder's daughter, whose groom too, was from India, had not been able to get along with him; that is why Rashim insisted on going to India to meet the boy herself. When Daljit and Simran also sided with their sister, Paramjit and Baldev had to give in.

Heaven knows what convinced Baldev, but he said, 'I think, Rashim is right. One must weigh everything carefully before getting married. We may keep the occasion simple, but we must not try and save money when it comes to the right selection of a groom. Kiranjit and Simran should accompany you and Rashim to India. It is not necessary that a groom selected by *Bhaji* will automatically be accepted by Rashim.'

They left for India a few days later.

The groom selected for Rashim by her *taya* and *tayee* was not only rejected by Rashim, he was not liked by others either. Rashim frankly told her *tayaji* that her outlook and views were completely different from the suggested groom's.

Yet, this had given them an opportunity to visit India. If nothing else, they had been able to see their village and meet family and friends after so many years. They toured Punjab for three weeks, and returned home.

On their return, they acquainted Baldev with their list of reproaches. Baldev Singh stoically heard out each and every one of their valid complaints.

'My daughter-in-law was visiting them for the first time. She was not even given a proper reception. Neither did anyone give her the customary welcoming amount. Ten rupees in the hands of Rashim and twenty to Simran – that is all they could muster for my children. This is about the immediate family, the other relatives were no better. In fact, they expected imported goods and other gifts from us.'

'Mum, first of all tell Daddy about the incident at the airport,' Simran prompted his mother but then began to narrate it himself.

'Daddy, the four thousand rupees you had given us came in very handy. Bikkar had come to the airport in a van. A friend of his, Pamma from Pasla village was with him. We came out of the airport in a hurry and thought that we would have the money changed the next day in the city. When we reached the village, Bikkar had a whispered conversation with Pamma who came to us and said, "*Bhaji*, the van driver is asking for two thousand rupees." I do not know what we would have done, had you not given us that amount.

'The snacks and tea during the trip was also paid for by us. Often Bikkar would take me to the city on his motorbike. There we would bump into his friends or relatives. We would drink beer and eat in some restaurant. Bikkar would buy liquor from the licence shop, or mutton, or some other groceries, but the payment was always from my pocket.

'When we were to leave, they knew that we had some seven to eight thousand rupees left. They had seen us put that money in a bag. After reaching Delhi, he finally asked us, "*Bhaji*, this money will not be of any use to you in England…"

'I said, "Of course, this will be of some use. We'll use it the way we used the four thousand rupees we had brought with us. This amount will come in handy during another visit."'

Sohan told Baldev that Rashim was right. It would not be easy to adjust with a groom from India. Buying the house itself would be a big chore. A locally settled groom would at least have his own house.

'Garewal's son is working as an accountant. I am sure your family will like that boy. Especially Rashim will find him suitable. If you allow me, I can talk to them. They are a very nice family.'

Thanks to Sohan Singh's mediatory skills, Rashim found a suitable life partner and Baldev Singh's family, good relatives. Everybody was happy. Both sides felt deeply indebted to Sohan Singh.

Chapter Eleven

Kulwinder had been sponsored twice by his relatives in England to attend weddings in the family. But each time he was denied visa as the consulate had found his replies to their questions unsatisfactory.

Eventually, he spoke to an agent who was in the business of sending people abroad. He had already taken money from about fifteen or twenty people with the promise to arrange papers for them. The deal was that three lakh rupees would be paid in advance and another two lakhs after reaching the destination. He had asked all his clients to reach his Jalandhar office on the evening on 25 November. From there, he would send them to the Delhi airport by a minibus.

When they reached Jalandhar on the given date, they were in for a shock. The office signboard was missing and there was a lock hanging on the door. The agent Ajaib Singh and his partner Behal Sahib had vanished into thin air.

In spite of having lost so much money, Kulwinder still had the craze for going abroad.

Two years later he approached another agent. This agent told him that he was organising a tourist group of ten members. Initially, the group would be sent to Thailand and from there to Italy. From Italy, they would go to either Germany or France. They might go to England from there, if they wished.

As instructed by the agent, they had torn up their passports before their arrival in Germany. They were given political asylum in Germany. This authorised them to work within a certain geographic area, or to claim unemployment benefits, if unable to find work.

After spending a year in Germany, Kulwinder somehow managed to visit England. Like Kulwinder, many others had used the excuse of terrorist activities in the Punjab and applied for political asylum. Asylum on this basis was being granted to a large number of people. Not just from India, from many other countries, too, people were using the subterfuge of political asylum to enter Europe or North America in search of a more prosperous life. Mrs Cheema's nephew Kulwinder was granted political asylum on the basis of the statement that 'the Indian police were after him'.

He was on dole, but also worked with a builder. On one hand he was fleecing the government, and on the other, he was making money without paying any tax. His paternal aunt would not charge him for boarding and lodging. That enabled him to save around three hundred pounds a week.

Once he received the permission to work, he left the earlier builder and joined another one. Within a year and a half he became an expert in carpentry and double glazing of windows.

After a while, Cheema's son asked Kulwinder to join him and they set up a building company of their own. They started their business under the name J & K, the initials of their names, Joginder and Kulwinder. They had made good contacts in one or two council offices. How to get the plans approved, how to apply for grants, which are the jobs entitled to grants – they had a good knowledge of all these matters. They were able to get a lot of contracts on the basis of grants in the areas which had a large concentration of Indians. Besides, they were doing non-grant jobs, too. Within a year or two their business began to flourish.

Countries like Britain reward the hard-working with economic success. Kulwinder was not only a diligent worker but also a handsome young man. Maybe that is why Ravinder's wife liked him. She broached the subject to Ravinder. 'Mrs Cheema's nephew is good-looking; he is also running his business successfully. He has even bought a house. There is just one apprehension – I have heard these men in the business of razing and building homes, are usually big boozers.'

'Everyone here drinks a little bit. The ones who do not probably have had enough to last a lifetime, before quitting. Very few strong-willed men have not succumbed to this habit. Even I drink, although I should quit now for health reasons. Tell me, which of our relatives does not drink?'

'Then, why don't you go and talk to Cheema *Bhaji* about Kulwinder?'

'But you should ask Pinkie first. What does she want? We cannot go against her wishes.'

'Does she think differently? She is my daughter. I know her mind more or less.'

'But I still think it would be better for her if she gets a partner who has been brought up in this country,' Ravinder argued.

'Kulwinder is not a bad guy either. His paternal aunt told me that he has done BA in India. By now, I am sure, he speaks English just like the ones who went to local schools here. Besides, Pinkie will have no relatives to deal with and will be able to enjoy life better. It is not easy to deal with mothers and sisters-in-law. I know how difficult it was for me to endure your family. And do not forget, it is not as if Pinkie is highly educated.'

'Do not thrust your own stories into this matter. Your son will also get married one day. Would you like the bride's parents to tell you that their daughter does not want to live with her in-laws? In that case what would you do? Leave the house or go and commit suicide?' Ravinder asked with obvious irritation.

'Stop fretting. We are not in a hurry. You may speak to them at leisure, and meanwhile get Pinkie's opinion also,' she said trying to placate Ravinder.

Pinkie and Kulwinder met each other and talked for a while. Kulwinder had no reservations but Pinkie asked for more time to think it over. They met a couple of times more at Kulwinder's paternal aunt's house. Pinkie laid bare everything like an open book: her thoughts, her way of life and her dreams for the future. Kulwinder could not open up the way Pinkie had.

The thought of setting up home with a beautiful girl like Pinkie was very appealing. Instead of trying to gauge her mind, Kulwinder concentrated on her body. *What is so special about the mind?* he thought. *If you possess someone's body, the mind is not going to run away.* In his traditional way of thinking, the mind was much less important than the body.

No doubt, Kulwinder was an industrious and appealing young man. Pinkie tried hard to understand what was in his mind. But if someone does not allow you to look inside, how would you get an idea?

Kulwinder was born and raised in India; Pinkie in England. Most, if not all, people raised in India do not say what is in their hearts. Their inner thoughts, more often than not, are not conveyed. But children brought up in England do not stand on ceremony on such serious occasions; they frankly convey what they feel.

However, their marriage was eventually settled.

As soon as the news reached Kulwinder's workers they asked for liquor and kebabs to celebrate. Some grant work had already begun in a Gujarati fellow's house. Kulwinder was in a hurry to finish that job before his wedding. The council had granted thirteen thousand pounds. After deducting all the expenses, Kulwinder and Joginder would still be left with five to six thousand pounds. Joginder was mostly at the building yard, while Kulwinder would attend the sites where work was in progress.

Instead of employing Najar and Dara as daily wagers, Kulwinder decided that it was better to get the foundation work done on contractual basis. Earlier too, whenever he was in a hurry, he had completed some small jobs on a contractual basis. Though Najar would get an amount equivalent to double the wages, the work would get finished in two days instead of four.

Although Najar was totally illiterate, he could understand the gist of the matter, when spoken to. While making the chimneys, Najar made some conversation in broken Hindi with the lady of the house. In the afternoon, Dara went away to buy chips for lunch.

By the time Dara returned with two cans of beer, burger and chips, Najar was sitting at Mrs Patel's dining table enjoying *papad*, chicken curry and hot rice. Mrs Patel was sitting in front of him, busy peeling vegetables.

One day while Najar was digging the foundation, Mrs Patel kept looking at his brawny body for a long time from behind the curtains. Physical work endows the body with a particular charm.

Before she left for school to fetch her children, Mrs Patel changed her dress and ignoring Dara's presence came up to Najar and said something to him in half-Hindi, half-Gujarati. Najar did not understand what she had said and looked questioningly at Dara.

Dara said, 'I think she is asking if she seems worthless to you.'

Najar was flustered. He looked at Mrs Patel but did not see anything except a smile in her eyes. There was no trace of any reproach on her face. Noticing that naughty smile in her eyes, Najar felt somewhat relieved and said, 'No, I have not said anything like that.'

But he felt that his words had dampened the joy that was earlier visible on Mrs Patel's face.

The following day, at a time when Najar was working alone, Mrs Patel came up to him and asked, 'Don't I look beautiful to you?'

'I never said you are not. You are indeed very beautiful. I lose my senses when I see you.'

'Then why did you say that you do not find me *ruri*?' Mrs Patel had used a word that meant 'rubbish' in Punjabi but obviously meant something entirely different in Gujarati.

'Oh! I did not understand what you were saying yesterday. That fellow Dara said something totally different.' Having said this, he took a step towards Mrs Patel but saw Kulwinder and Dara enter with two more labourers from the side entrance.

Chapter Twelve

After their marriage, Pinkie began to think that her parents had indeed found her a suitable partner. Pinkie and Kulwinder were very happy with each other.

After finishing work in the evening, Kulwinder would have some beer with his friends and come home. If he felt like drinking more, he would have a peg of whisky to go with his dinner. Sometimes he would implore Pinkie to give him company, and make a mild drink for her. But Pinkie did not enjoy anything except wine. Gradually, he started getting wine for her.

Pinkie was quite concerned about Kulwinder's increasing size of the belly. She told him that she did not like people with paunches. For that reason she restrained herself from drinking wine on a regular basis. From experience she knew that after consuming alcohol, people were inclined to eat twice their normal amount and then fall asleep immediately after, without having digested the food properly.

Their marriage was barely six or seven months old, when Pinkie began to feel that there was something lacking in their life. She began to feel dissatisfied with her daily routine of cooking and washing dishes after coming home from work, and then retiring to bed.

Kulwinder too, became more temperamental and moody as time went by. He began to come home late after spending long evenings with his friends in the pub. Sometimes, he would arrive after having already eaten, while Pinkie would still be waiting for him for dinner at home. On such days he would arrive and immediately retire to the bedroom.

In course of time, his friends began to visit him at home also. They would open a bottle of drink and settle in the drawing room, soon after their arrival. Whenever Kulwinder asked Pinkie to make an omelette or prepare some chicken dish for them, Pinkie would feel as if she was a mere waitress, who was simply given orders.

For a while she did everything without complaining. However, by and by she began to criticise Kulwinder for returning home late everyday, or for going to bed late or about the ill-mannered ways in which his friends ate and drank in their house. At times, Pinkie would leave the dirty dishes on the table and go off to sleep.

She also began to openly complain to her parents about Kulwinder's misdeeds.

Pinkie's mother would say, 'Do not take these things to heart. Such happenings are a part of life. Your daddy also used to bring his friends over. You have seen all that...'

'Mummy, because I have seen all that, I detest it all the more. I cannot live like you. Why should I cook for so many people?'

Pinkie's parents would visit the young couple, sit with them and advise them to be patient with each other, but Pinkie would stick to the position that she was not at fault in any way. While Kulwinder would blame Pinkie for everything.

Hoping to resolve the issue they decided to discuss the problem with Piara Singh Cheema and his wife. After all, this issue was of equal concern to the Cheema family, too.

Everyone tried his or her best. They implored the young couple to think of their coming child, and try to live happily with each other like they had earlier.

Pinkie gave birth to a very beautiful child. Everyone hoped that his arrival would set everything right. As everyone had expected, a marked change did take place in Kulwinder's behaviour.

He would play with his son Raju as soon as he arrived home. Even if he was upset with Pinkie over something, he would never let go of the pleasure of playing with his son before going off to sleep.

Sometimes, while Pinkie would still be cleaning the kitchen, an inebriated Kulwinder would pick up his son and go to the bedroom. One day, by the time Pinkie reached their bedroom upstairs, Kulwinder was fast asleep and snoring loudly while young Raju was playing by himself. Pinkie was furious and said, 'What if the child had fallen from the bed?'

The atmosphere of their house had become unpredictable – at times pleasant, at other times, unpleasant.

Meanwhile Raju completed two years. His second birthday was celebrated in a grand manner, but a big fight took place the same night between Kulwinder and Pinkie.

On the night of the birthday party, Kulwinder danced with a friend of Pinkie's while singing along with the song playing in the background, 'I have hooked a golden lass...' But when the friend's husband got up to dance with Pinkie, Kulwinder, beside himself with jealousy, smashed his beer glass against the table, splashing those near the table.

Time went by at its given pace. Time does not stop for anything or anyone. It is a river flowing eternally. Some of us are on one bank of this river called time, while some others are across, on the other bank. Some of us march with it, while others are left behind.

Raju was three and half years old now; their domestic bickering was four.

Many times Pinkie tried to compromise and tried to live like her mother, forgetting and tolerating everything. But

75

she was unable to do that for long.

Then she realised that she was getting caught in the web of a male-dominated society, a society in which her mother had been deeply enmeshed. She decided to find the courage to gnaw through these entanglements and free herself. She wanted to lead life on her own terms, not on someone else's terms as her mother had done.

Eventually their marriage ended in a divorce.

When matters reached a head, all around tongues started wagging. Someone would say, 'Gone are the days when children arrived here after having been brought up in India. Those children listened to their parents and kept their mouths shut. But the children born and brought up in England cannot be like them.'

Someone else would add, 'These children who go to school and interact with the whites have very different ideas. They consider marriage to be their private affair and nothing to do with their family.'

'We cannot force our children into anything,' someone else would demur.

'Times have changed. Besides, we are in another country. Parents have oppressed their children for long in India. Now, it is the turn of the children to assert themselves. They are the decision-makers now.'

'Besides, if we try to look at things from their point of view, they are not doing anything wrong. We tend to think they are wrong because we look at them and judge them from our own point of view. That is what we are used to, judging others with our own perceptions.'

Everyone offered their own opinion, judging things from their own perspective.

Chapter Thirteen

A month had passed since the elections had taken place at the Court Road gurdwara. But the occasional visitors were still congratulating the newly elected president.

Inside the hall, the devotees were being urged to contribute money for buying the land adjacent to the gurdwara. With the increase in the number of devotees, it had become imperative to build a new dining hall and a car park. The factory next door, owned by a Jewish family had closed down. The new committee was very keen to buy this space.

The committee had already met Mr Cohen twice over the last twenty days. Moved by the Sikh spirit of the committee members, Mr Cohen said, 'Look Mr Singh, I had no plans of selling this factory space. But persuaded by your devotion to your religion I might consider it. However, I have to consult my family first. Only then I'll be able to tell you anything. Please meet me again next Monday at noon. I'll let you know of our decision regarding the sale.'

Sitting in the gurdwara office, President Gajjan Singh conferred with other committee members. 'If we manage to conclude this deal, you maybe rest assured that nobody will be able to trounce us in the next elections. Now the question is how to get hold of the requisite amount. Swaran Singh has great regard for Jagir Singh. The other day he had agreed to donate five thousand pounds. If you, Jagir Singh, manage to convince him to donate ten thousand pounds instead, then many other donators will be ready to contribute bigger amounts.

'Swaran Singh is such a big businessman. Besides he is truly devoted to the cause of the gurdwara. We will inscribe the names of the contributors on a marble plaque and install that at the main entrance. Please go to his house this evening and talk to him. Give me a call after that. We'll begin the list with his name.'

'All right, I'll try to convince him. But Mota Singh should also try and persuade his fellow villager. He has a flourishing business in clothing and dabbles in millions. Sometimes spurred by their acclaim, people agree to loosen their purse strings,' Jagir Singh offered this tip indicating the treasurer, Mota Singh.

'They may have business worth millions or even billions. But what matters in the end is how big their heart is. They are not the kind to be taken in by acclaim or praise. They cannot even offer a cup of tea to a visitor, how will they contribute any money? One should not have expectations of getting milk from an ox.'

After reaching home, Mr Cohen discussed the matter with his wife, 'Some people from the Sikh temple had come to visit me today. They are extremely keen on buying the land where our factory is. Their devotion and religious sentiments may make them ready to pay a higher price. You tell me, how much should we ask for?'

Then without having waited for her reply, he continued, 'I think if we ask for ninety thousand pounds, we maybe able to clinch the deal at eighty thousand pounds.'

'But the other day you were saying that the agent thinks we may not get more than forty thousand pounds,' asked his wife, a bit intrigued.

'Yes, the agent had said that there was no buyer ready to pay more than forty thousand pounds. But now neither is there an agent in between, nor are they ordinary buyers. Now the Sikh community is buying the land for a gurdwara.

It is being bought collectively, with the money collected from the donors.' Having said this he began to laugh loudly and added, 'Let me tell you something else. The devotion of these people is very great.'

'All right, in that case you may try and ask for ninety thousand pounds,' Mrs Cohen expressed her agreement.

The opponents spread rumours that delegations from the local temple and the mosque had also visited Mr Cohen. Since there has been a substantial increase in the number of Bangladeshis in the area, they were looking out for a plot to build their mosque. They had no dearth of resources, as the money would come in from the Arab countries.

As soon as they heard this, Gajjan Singh called up Jagir Singh and Mota Singh. They decided to meet at home instead of convening a meeting in the gurdwara. All of them agreed that if they do not manage to procure this plot for constructing a dining hall and a car park, it would be a matter of shame, indeed. They conferred with four or five influential members of their group about this problem and implored them in the name of religion to help out. Eventually it was decided to offer a hundred thousand pounds to Mr Cohen for the plot, and even pay five to seven thousand extra, if necessary.

Jagir Singh suggested that the factory should not be demolished after acquisition. By removing the walls between the cutting room and the main factory, the area could be remodelled into a large dining hall with kitchen. The money that would be required for demolition and then reconstruction could be used more judiciously to acquire the land.

The main question was of pride and self-esteem. If the Moslems manage to get hold of this land, it would be very unfortunate. A mosque right beside the gurdwara would mean constant feuds between the communities. The Moslems do not bring their womenfolk to the mosque;

hence they would gape at Sikh women all the time.

Through the 'espionage' services of Kehar Singh, this news reached the opposing group overnight. Hearing of the latest preoccupation of the current Gurdwara Committee, the ex-president Bikkar Singh clapped gleefully and remarked, 'How naive these fellows are! Someone should jolt them out of their stupor and ask a simple question. Do they really think that the Moslems are as stupid as they themselves are? Why would they want to build their mosque right next to a gurdwara?'

At the designated time, a party of five Sikh representatives arrived to meet Mr Cohen. Since Jagir Singh had earlier worked as a teacher, his English was comparatively better. It was decided that he would initiate the dialogue.

Jagir Singh began without any preamble, 'Look, Mr Cohen! We do not wish to waste either your time or our own. We know that probably some other people have also approached you. They are not interested in buying the land; their objective is to spoil the deal. Besides, no one else will be able to match the price we are ready to pay you. That is because this land is right next to the gurdwara. We would not offer even one fourth of this amount, if this plot was located elsewhere.'

Seeking confirmation from the members of their party and addressing the president he added, 'So, shall we disclose our offer to Mr Cohen?'

'Yes, yes. There is no one in a position to bid more than us? Mr Cohen will certainly accept our offer,' two or three voices said in unison.

'Mr Cohen, we are keen to finalise the deal without any further beating around the bush. Our maximum and last offer is – a hundred thousand pounds.' Having said this Jagir Singh and company tried to gauge a 'yes' or 'no' from Mr Cohen's face.

Mr Cohen was hoping for seventy to eighty thousand at

the most. Cloaking his delight he said with a deadpan expression, 'You are buying this yard for a religious purpose, so I will not be uncompromising. I respect your religion like I respect my own. But I never take a decision all by myself. I'd like to call my wife and seek her approval.'

'Why not? By all means. Please call her right away.'

Mr Cohen dialled a number and spoke to his wife for a couple of minutes in Hebrew. As soon as he put down the receiver, Gajjan Singh and the other members of the party looked expectantly at Mr Cohen.

Mr Cohen put on a solemn face and began to doodle on a piece of paper on the table. To break the uneasy silence Gajjan Singh asked anxiously, 'What is your decision then, Mr Cohen?'

'The fact is that my wife does not want a penny less than a hundred and ten thousand pounds. I have even requested her to consider it in the name of religion.'

For a while Jagir Singh and his comrades discussed the matter amongst themselves in Punjabi. Mr Cohen merely watched their unintelligible conversation. He knew that the net he had cast was unlikely to return empty.

Then all of them made as if to leave, indicating their impatience. 'Throw another five thousand on the bastard's face,' said Gajjan Singh to his friends in Punjabi. At last, Jagir Singh began to renegotiate. 'Mr Cohen, you have mentioned religion. We hope you will accept our offer of a hundred and five thousand pounds. We are not in a position to offer more than that.'

Mr Cohen did not say anything and began dialling again. This time he spoke to his wife in English. 'Please accept it now. These people are ready to pay a hundred and five thousand pounds. After all they are doing it for their religion. A sacrifice for the sake of religion.' Then he put down the receiver, with a smile on his face and said, 'All right, your offer has been accepted. I will pray that your

81

religion spreads and flourishes.'

Mr Cohen shook hands with them over the amicable conclusion of the deal and both parties took down the names and addresses of each other's solicitors.

Thereafter, they went straight to a pub. They felt satisfied at having accomplished the task and sat down in a corner with their glasses of beer, discussing further measures to be taken to collect the requisite amount for the gurdwara. From the pub, they moved over to the house of the president. There too, the subject of collection campaign dominated their conversation over pegs of whisky.

Monetary constraints may cause a lone family or a person to suspend his plans, but a common cause is not hindered by these considerations. When people join hands for a cause, they can collect as much money as they wish to. This has always been the case, and probably will remain so in the future, too.

Chapter Fourteen

After the closure of many foundries in Birmingham and other areas of the Midlands, a large number of uneducated immigrants from Punjab were rendered jobless. They belonged to the age group of fifty to sixty years, and were not equipped to take up other jobs.

Many of those who were in the habit of drinking five or seven glasses of beer every evening had begun to brew liquor at home. Then there were many on dole, with very little family income, who could no longer afford afternoon visits to the pub and were forced to visit gurdwaras instead. Some of them began to grow a beard and wear a turban. Similarly, in 1971, the frequent and impressive appearance of the victorious General Arora of the Indian army in the media influenced many others to wear the turban as a fashion statement.

Daulati's brother had left Midland and settled in East London. Sometimes, in an inebriated state he would say, 'Sohan Singh, my friend, please do not mind my words, but I think you Londoners live like urbanites. We, from Midland, are used to living like village folk. You tell us to speak softly inside a pub, and to wear neckties. But we are used to shouting and singing in the pubs. We do not even remember how a tie is knotted.'

'Mangat Ram, you think we are urbanites. Yet, Mr Gulati accuses us of being plain villagers. This brother of yours, Daulati, also thinks that we are villagers just because he has lived in Ambala. You have come to England from a town that was as good as any city. What makes you brand us as urbanites?'

Although Daulati had already gone on pension, he was still very agile. Mangat Ram and Daulati joined hands and, with the help of their family, set up a garment business in East London. Their children had a knack for business; their wives, too, quickly learnt the tricks of the trade.

After a while, they bought another shop adjoining theirs and set up a factory at the back and a warehouse in the front. They also hired three or four Indian men and about fifteen Punjabi women to work in their establishment.

By adopting the practice of piecework and piece rate, they were able to increase their profits. One woman would sew the collars, another would stitch the zips, and yet another would take care of the pockets. They were paid according to the quality and quantity of work done. Some hard-working women worked ten-hour shifts on all seven days and took home as much as the men did. But on paper most of the women were shown as part-time workers. That way both parties had to pay less tax.

Later, they decreased the number of sewing machines in their factory and allowed the workers to stitch at home. In many families, even the husbands and children learnt basic stitching, and began to lend a hand to their womenfolk in their spare time.

Many girls were even compelled by their greedy mothers to help them out after returning from school. These girls were not in a position to say 'no' to their mothers, yet, at the same time were not ready to suffer the daily drudgery. Most of them were forced to lead dual lives – one in their school and outside their homes, and a completely different one at home. In spite of living in a very liberal country, they were not free to wear clothes of their choice. On the other hand, their brothers enjoyed much more freedom.

On account of their gender, the values of Indian society were still being forced on them. Incensed by this injustice, many girls had raised the banner of revolt. As such, the parents began to suffer because of the problems they had created themselves. However, one could not blame the parents either; they were doing what they thought was best. The parents were like uninformed and innocent children, and their children were even more so. Under the circumstances, the inadvertent parental injustice towards children appeared almost cruel.

As time went by, video made its appearance in homes. Films became the main source of entertainment. Indian girls were much impressed watching the beautiful heroines clad in elegant dresses or saris. Glamour was weaving its magical spell. Girls, who were not seen in Indian dresses outside their homes earlier, now began to flaunt their native attire on the roads. This led to a considerable demand for garment shops.

It was a Sunday evening on a clear summer day. Baldev had invited his friend Sohan Singh over to his house. He wanted to discuss something important – something that he had heard from his wife Paramjit. Paramjit also worked as a seamstress in Daulati's factory. She had heard many co-workers whisper among themselves with the intention that it should reach her ears. At least that was the impression she had gathered.

Daulati's daughter and Sohan Singh's son were in the same college. During lunch break the women workers seemed to have nothing better to do then to gossip about this young pair's affair. Their conversation would continue in the following pattern:

'Their parents already know each other well. Now the children will cement it into a relationship,' one of them would mention.

'Shh... keep quiet, if you want to continue working here,' the other one would advise.

All of them knew that this affair was not likely to culminate into a union as the families belonged to different castes and religions. However, this liaison would bring shame to the families and entertain the bystanders while it lasted.

Pouring a second peg of whisky, Baldev Singh began, 'Sohan Singh, at times there is hardly any basis for concern, but people blow it out of proportion. Or you may say, matters get blown up.'

Hearing this, Sohan Singh burst into laughter. 'Did you meet Nirmala recently?' he asked.

'No, I have not met Nirmala. But do you know what I am...'

'Of course, I know. If a friend would not understand what his friend is alluding to, who would?' Having said this he began to laugh again. After that he consumed half of his drink and began, 'Look! I was about to tell you. The friendship between my son Balwinder and Daulati's daughter Simi has turned into a full-fledged affair now. I do not know for how long they have been carrying on secretly! He did not even let his father know. Once I caught them together and that is when he confessed that both of them have similar ideas and common interests. Maybe people will think that I am ignoring the caste factor because of Daulati's millions. But you know me, and you know their family, too.

'You know I am not the kind to be bothered by what people say or think. Daulati maybe a millionaire, but I am not interested in receiving anything from the girl's side. I'll go in for a simple wedding. Now, on the question of caste, people may say anything, call them lower caste or whatever. But you know that theirs is a mixed family of Hindus and Sikhs. They have been running tailoring shops. Tailoring is not worse than collecting night soil. You cannot stop the wagging tongues, people will say whatever they want to—'

'Damn the people!' Baldev did not let Sohan finish the sentence. 'They have fifteen *Jutt* women working in their factory, like labourers who used to work in our fields back home. What did we pay our workers? Nothing. But these fellows pay them weekly wages. Our womenfolk are working under them. In India I have seen *Jutt* families who lived worse than the so-called lower castes. Everything boils down to economics in the end. Who is a *Jutt* and who is a *chamar* from a lower caste? Everyone is a mere worker here. Do you find any difference between people?'

'Baldev Singh, if I were the kind to differentiate between people on the basis of their caste, would I agree to this marriage?'

'What does Nirmala have to say?'

'She is a bit reluctant right now. Her brothers are instigating her. After all they are the maternal uncles of the groom. They say that a *Jutt* needs to be matched with a *Jutt* only.'

'Pick up your glass. Nirmala should not dare to decline this match. Paramjit and I will make her agree. And you know how mothers are! A little coercion by the son, and the mother is ready to accede. Usually it is more difficult to make a father like you give his consent. The unyielding *Jutt* in him does not surrender easily. But now that the *Jutt* in you is ready, getting the assent from the boy's maternal uncles will not be all that difficult. I am proud of friends like you. To tell you the truth Sohan Singh, you are really a great man.'

Baldev shouted for Paramjit and called her from the kitchen, 'You have seen and known this man for years. But you do not know what a great man he is. Go now and prepare some really nice food for us.' So saying, he burst into lines from a song:

     I would not let you know
 .   I would sit and cry
     Right beside you
     But would not bare my soul
     I would not let you know
     My love…

'*Bhaji*, I think he is a bit drunk today.'

'It is not the liquor, I am drunk with bliss today. Bliss, induced by a happy news…'

Chapter Fifteen

Paramjit and Baldev tried their best to convince Nirmala but she remained adamant and refused to budge from the position she had taken. She said that Amrik *Bhaji* was the final authority and she would go by his decision.

Baldev told her that he was glad that Nirmala had such high regard for her elder brother, but she must think about her son's happiness, too. He reminded her that she had always maintained that Balwinder's happiness was her prime concern. Hence, anyone coming in the way of his love and happiness should not be the arbiter.

'But, *Bhaji*, you are a wise man. We are from the *Jutt* community; they are *chhimbas*, a much lower caste of tailors. What will the people say? How can we explain this to our community?'

'Tell me honestly, is your community really bothered about you? How often have the people from your community or your village stepped out to help you at the time of need? Your community is not going to help you either sow or reap your fields. We may not even go back to our country. But, we know for sure that we have to live here. Over a period of time, not merely our community, but our values will also change. Discuss the matter with Sohan Singh and your children. You are the best judge of your family's situation; no one else can take a better decision on your behalf.

'Besides, do you know what is the name of Daulati's younger brother in Delhi? He is Sarup Singh, a full-fledged Sikh, and you know that the true Sikh of the guru should be above caste and community. Mangat Ram has two brothers-in-law; both are turbaned Sikhs. So is his father-in-law. In fact, we are the ones who rarely go to the gurdwara. You know that Sarla and her family go there regularly every Sunday.'

Having said this, Baldev closed the door behind him and left. Nirmala stayed back in the hall, pondering over what she had been told. She felt that there was some truth in Baldev's reasoning.

Barely a month after this talk, Nirmala received a call from her elder brother, Amrik. In a weary voice he asked, 'So, Nimmi. What have you people decided about Balwinder's marriage?'

'What decision, *Bhaji*? You know the father-son duo. Both are very happy. In fact, I have heard from a couple of people that everyone has been blaming me behind my back.'

'Well, if everyone is happy with this alliance, then why should we object to it? Our main concern should be Balwinder's well-being.'

'But you are the one who said that our community will never accept this alliance. I was sticking to my position only because of you.' Nirmala sent the ball back to her brother's court.

'Nimmi, after all we are not marrying off our daughter to someone out of caste. We are from the boy's side and whatever the girl may or may not be, she is a Punjabi girl. Many of our boys have been marrying Gujarati or white girls. This alliance is certainly better than that.'

Nirmala's brothers were the last obstacle. Once they agreed, Nirmala too, relented. Both sides began to discuss dates suitable for the betrothal and wedding ceremonies.

On the day of the registration, Sohan Singh had wanted to arrange a small party in his home. But on Daulati's suggestion, it was fixed in Mangat Ram's new house. That way, the house warming for Mangat's new home could also be taken care of.

Only close relatives and friends as well as the friends of Balwinder and Simi were invited to the party.

Nirmala's brothers were stunned by the opulence and extravagance displayed at Mangat Ram's house. Nirmala's sisters-in-law were equally overwhelmed by all the pomp. Probably they had never been to such a spacious and affluent home.

'This chutney is very tasty. Otherwise, you get merely boiled jaggery these days, making the chutney too sweet,' Balwinder's aunt said.

'Of course, only salty chutney goes well with pakoras. What is the point of putting sugary balls in a salty solution as they often do these days?' added another aunt.

Baldev nudged Sohan Singh and said, 'I think your brothers-in-law are still not happy. Instead of enjoying themselves they seem to be sulking.'

'No, that is not the case. You see that girl with puffed hair? She had eloped with a Moslem boy. That is why they are looking slightly embarrassed.'

'Oh! Now I understand what made them relent and accept this alliance. Earlier they would only talk of their pride in their higher caste.'

'Baldev Singh, circumstances make a man reasonable. If the circumstances are beyond your control, you learn to make compromises.'

Baldev Singh gestured towards Amrik Singh and his two brothers to come and sit next to them. They came up and joined Baldev and Sohan. Everyone around was busy eating and enjoying the party. After the feast, children switched on the TV. It was time for the news. Hearing the news of seven thousand dead in Mexico, Sohan Singh signalled the children to keep quiet for a moment. A mother was wailing over her six- or seven-year-old dead child in her lap. Another young girl was crying loudly over the dead bodies of her parents. Another visual showed an old man with tearful eyes leaning against a wall. Baldev Singh and Sohan Singh were also moved to tears. They were carefully listening, trying to understand what had happened. Meanwhile, Amrik Singh shouted at the children to switch off the telly and they did that.

Sohan Singh and Baldev Singh kept quiet, although they were keen to hear the detailed news. Gradually, the music moved on to songs with faster beats. Women began to dance the *giddha*. The betrothal party was in full swing.

Chapter Sixteen

It was decided to demolish the building adjacent to the Court Road gurdwara and rebuild it. The enthusiasm of the devotees was to be seen to be believed. Many artisans and craftsmen offered their services for free. Many others agreed to work for the construction activities at half rate. One builder gifted ten trucks of concrete and two hundred sacks of cement. Another one promised to give bricks and woodblocks at half rate.

When Moga builders committed themselves to constructing the dining hall and kitchen on a turnkey basis for a mere twenty-eight thousand pounds, the hall, full of devotees went ecstatic and spiritedly raised religious slogans. Everyone thought it to be a very cheap deal – who else could offer to construct such a large hall with tiles and fittings included in the cost for such an amount?

But the devotees were bewildered when they were told that the contract for building the hall has been passed on to someone else and that too, for forty-two thousand pounds.

People began making varied accusations. Some said that even the first builder would have made eight thousand pounds at least from the proposed twenty-eight thousand pounds. Someone else said that the new builder would make twelve thousand instead of eight thousand and the remaining ten thousand would also go to different pockets.

'So what, my friend? This is business. People do business to make money, that is why they run around. Do any of you have time to spare for charity?'

'The donators will continue to donate. The appropriators will continue to appropriate. That is the way of life,' someone else added his bit.

'But, I must say, there is one remarkable thing about the Sikhs. Wherever they have settled in this wide world, they have always built first of all, a gurdwara to take care of the boarding and lodging of the travellers. I had reached England with great difficulty, and penniless. Had it not been for the gurdwara, I would have gone hungry and homeless. Have you ever seen any temple or mosque doing such service? You'll neither get a place to stay there nor food to eat.'

'Who knows, maybe temples and mosques, too provide shelter and food. You have not gone there to check for yourself, have you?' said someone standing nearby.

'No, I know that they do not have such provisions.'

Before Balwinder got married, one day both Mangat Ram and Daulat Ram along with Baldev Singh visited Sohan Singh. Sohan Singh was already aware of the purpose of their visit. After a while Daulati asked Balwinder to fetch Simi, too. It would be better if everyone participated and a decision could be taken collectively.

They sat in the lounge drinking tea. At last, Daulati broached the subject. 'Like all parents I want that our children should be obedient, and I am sure you, too, wish the same. All of us wish for an amiable and harmonious atmosphere in our homes. Nobody wants divisions and disagreements in the family. But at times, differences arise because of our near and dear ones. Our own relatives, in-laws, brothers or sisters-in-law, or sometimes even our friends or neighbours, I have often seen, that people who want peace in their own homes are not averse to creating trouble in other people's families.

'But the whites are not like this; they are not jealous of others the way we are. This disease is peculiar to us. Maybe gradually we'll also discard this tendency. Now, to cut a long story short, I want to tell my daughter in the presence of all, that from now onwards you will be her parents. I would like to tell Balwinder the same that both of you have to live together following the wishes of your parents, and maintaining the unity and prosperity of your joint family. Now, I have one more request. Please do not take it otherwise. The rest I leave to Baldev Singh.'

Daulati finished what he was saying and gestured towards Baldev Singh.

'To avoid any misunderstanding or misinterpretation, Daulat Ram has already shared his modest request with me. He was a bit unsure about how you people may take it, as he does not want you to think that he is proud of his wealth. Or that he wants the young couple to move out. That is not the intent of either Daulati or Mangat Ram.

'I am amazed at Daulati's humility; even while giving he is afraid of hurting the pride of the person he is giving to. There is no dearth of affluent people who do not hesitate grabbing if they can, and are not averse to receiving whatever comes their way. There are also some, who give and are vain to the extreme, unlike Daulati.

'Well, the sum and substance is that Daulati is worried that if he, keeping in mind the future of the young couple, decides to gift them a certain amount, you may take it otherwise. Not that he is worried about their future, but still… These brothers believe that each child must get a share of their parental property. That is why they wish to transfer the two-bedroom house on Leamington Road in their name. Who knows, they may require a separate home after a while once they have children. I request all of you not to say anything and we will infer your answer from your silence.' Having said this he gestured towards Balwinder and Simi and said cheerfully, 'Come on folks. Get us some beer at least.'

'Uncle, today we won't give you the fizzy can beer. We'll

treat you to draught beer from the cask in a pub. I am taking you to a countryside pub in the midst of fields,' Balwinder said.

'But when are you taking us?' Sohan Singh asked. 'It is almost eight o'clock already.'

'We are ready, Dad. My friends are waiting in their cars outside.'

Chapter Seventeen

Sohan Singh's friends were insistent that he throw a party to celebrate the birth of his grandson. When Baldev Singh, too, insisted on it, Sohan Singh said, 'You know that I do not believe in such ceremonies or traditions.'

Baldev would not let him go so easily, 'You have received forty thousand pounds as redundancy compensation. What are you going to do with that money? In fact, now you owe us a double party. You have to spend this amount. You cannot escape.'

'But don't you think this is simply showing off and a waste of money?'

'One should not be so rigid; some flexibility is called for at times. You are not going to carry the money over to the next world with you. If one does not have the means to celebrate, that is another matter altogether. But if you have the money, there is no harm in organising a bit of fun. Nirmala has already challenged me that I'll never be able to convince you, as you are the communist type. You are by no yardstick a communist – your family members do not even know that! I am the only one who knows your real worth. People like you are actually "the tail" that wags with the dog. Come, let us go and check out the hall next to the school. It has a seating capacity for about a hundred. That should suffice.'

Sohan Singh was left with no room for dilly-dallying any more after this.

When they went to Court Road gurdwara to borrow some large vessels for the party they noticed five or six men sunning themselves sitting next to the wall. Seeing Balbir and Gurbakhsh in that assemblage, Sohan could not resist saying, 'How interesting, dear comrades, one is a Naxalite while the other a Marxist. How come you have graced the gurdwara? You were the ones calling the Granth Sahib a mere book. You were unaware of the wisdom contained in the pages of that book then, and I do not think you are aware of it even now. But it is all right; the doors of the guru's house are open to all. You are also welcome to partake of the free community meal three times a day. You shirkers cannot work even if offered a job now...'

'Why are you after us? You are no different from us. Has anyone stopped you from partaking *langar*?' Balbir was getting angry.

'That is absolutely right, Balbir Singh. I am a hypocrite like you. So, please do not mind what I say. I am merely saying that whatever we maybe, if along with that we become slightly human too, it would be wonderful.'

'Do we not look human to you? Do you think we are horses?' Balbir was even more irritated.

'No, no. You certainly do not look like horses. But since you are short, you certainly look like that animal that resembles a horse but is slightly shorter.' Everyone around began to laugh at Sohan Singh's sly joke, while Gurbakhsh and company had to swallow their anger.

Meanwhile Mota Singh arrived, and as he was getting out of his car, one of them mentioned, 'Welcome, Mota Singh. You have had a really long trip to India this time!'

'No, it was not all that long. I stayed there only for five weeks. My wife insisted on sending Nindi along with me. She thinks that I do not keep well because at times my sugar level suddenly goes down. Nindi wanted to get back to England soon. Otherwise, I could have stayed there for another three or four weeks, or maybe I would have stayed there forever.'

Having said this, Mota Singh looked at the listeners to

gauge their reactions.

'Mota Singh, this is something that is beyond our obtuse brains,' Balbir Singh said abashed.

'No, Balbir Singh. It is quite simple and straightforward like you,' said Mota Singh, and joined in the laughter.

'By sending Nindi with me, my wife managed to get her husband back. You see, what had happened was that one evening Nindi went to town with my nephew. Since they had a car at their disposal, they used to roam around all the time. Suddenly that evening my sugar level went very low. I lost consciousness. And behold! My brother told everyone that I was dead – dead of a heart attack.' Mota Singh's recount kept everyone's attention glued to him, eager to know what happened next.

'So, my friends, I was laid down in the veranda, covered with a white sheet, just like a dead body. All this I heard the next day from Amru Mirasi, the village jester. Someone said that they should wait for the arrival of my son from town. Someone else mentioned that the sun was about to set and the funeral logs were lying ready in the funeral area. My brother was ready to cremate me saying that he would explain everything to my son on his return.

'Would you believe it, even the *Granthi* came to recite the final prayers. He even said those prayers for my departed soul. It was Amru Mirasi who noticed and said that my heart was still beating and I was perhaps moving under that damned white sheet. But my brother said that the sheet seemed to be moving because of the breeze from the ceiling fan. Our *Granthi*, with a scarf around his neck and his hands on his paunch mentioned that he had already recited the last prayers for the departed soul.

'After that they made a bier, put me on it and began their march to the cremation place, with a boy walking in front with a ceremonial gong to announce my departure to the other world. Our procession had barely crossed the outer peripheral road of the village when my son, Nindi arrived. When he asked who had died he was told that it was his unfortunate father who had died of a heart attack. Nindi asked them to put down the bier at once. But they would not do that. Two or three fellows caught hold of Nindi saying that the poor boy was beside himself with grief over his father's sudden death. However, Nindi did not give up. When he threatened them that he would call the police, they relented and put the bier down.

'Nindi noticed that my heart was still beating and immediately took me to the nearest hospital. There I was put on a glucose drip and regained consciousness soon after. The following day I asked my brother why they were in a hurry to get rid of me in this manner? He knew that I had already made a decision to bequeath my six fields to him. But I'll not do that now. I may leave the property to a gurdwara, but I will not let my brother get it. That is what happened, my friends.'

'What do you think, friends? Could this really have happened or has our treasurer concocted an anecdote to amuse us?' Balbir asked the fellows sitting next to him.

'I think it is a complete fabrication,' said Gurbakhsh Singh.

'There is no such thing as love for siblings left in this world. All relationships these days are based on need and greed,' said an old man sitting in a corner, ignoring what Balbir had said.

'This is not about siblings alone. In future, even our children will refuse to look after us.'

'But, why blame the children? Life has become so fast. They cannot support us at the cost of their own work. These days it is better to keep oneself in perfect health and not depend on others at all,' another fellow sitting there, expressed his opinion.

'What shall we do, Sohan Singh? If this is the state of

affairs, maybe we should drop the idea of celebrating the boy's birthday?' Baldev's comment made everyone laugh.

Perhaps it was a Saturday or a Sunday. In the Court Road gurdwara, a display of fireworks was scheduled for seven in the evening. It was being said that almost five hundred pounds had been spent to arrange the display.

Children and women everywhere were getting ready to watch the fascinating fireworks. At that time Daulati called up. He informed that the programme in the gurdwara was bound to be cancelled. He invited everyone over to his house instead. So that all of them could spend the evening together.

'But, what has happened?' Baldev Singh was anxious to know the reason behind the likely cancellation.

'Haven't you watched TV today? In the six o'clock news they said that a jumbo jet has crashed into the sea. Besides, forty-five thousand have been killed in an earthquake in Armenia. Haven't you seen the pictures on TV? You can watch it in the next bulletin. Which religious place is going to display fireworks on a day when so many have died? The people already congregated in the gurdwara may now pay their homage to the dead, and depart.'

But the children were still insistent on visiting the gurdwara. Sohan Singh suggested to Baldev to call up the gurdwara president at home and find out. If the programme had not been cancelled, the children and the women could go and watch it.

'Sohan Singh, what is the point in calling up? After a disaster of such magnitude can anyone be so dumb as to burst crackers? Do you think that is possible?'

'Don't be so sentimental, my friend. Just call up and find out.'

Baldev called up, and he was in for a surprise. The president's voice boomed through the receiver, '...cancelling a programme that has already been fixed is not so simple...'

Baldev Singh began to ponder aloud. 'The concept of Khalsa as visualised by Guru Gobind Singhji was not this...'

'But, in many ways the role of gurdwaras is commendable, too. They have done some admirable jobs. We may consider ourselves to be the flag bearers of Punjabi language, but the truth of the matter is that had it not been for the gurdwaras, we would not have been able to teach our children Punjabi. All who sent their children to the gurdwara are fortunate that their next generation is able to read and write Punjabi. They can correspond in Punjabi.

'The other area is that of sports. It was not easy to organise kabaddi tournaments of Punjab on English soil. Gurdwaras were the first to organise such events, and now they have become commonplace. We cannot deny the role of gurdwaras in these matters. Although, one must admit that we Sikhs are very unfortunate on one point. We are always divided over matters of political and religious beliefs. That has been our bane and other parties have always made use of this shortcoming in us.'

'Sohan Singh, we have a good insight into ourselves since we know our society from within. We do not like the division in gurdwaras on the basis of caste and community as our gurus condemned such differentiation. I do not know which heritage are we talking about, since we do not even follow the path shown by our gurus. Maybe, other religions are no better than ours, and are similarly divided.'

Chapter Eighteen

Those who are free from economic hardship, lead a peaceful and relaxed family life, do not indulge in excessive drinking or drug abuse, and are unlikely to fall ill easily. Usually they live a long and healthy life. Gajjan Singh had arrived in England from a similarly well-to-do family.

He was a strong man and was good at work. By nature he was very cheerful and a great raconteur. He secured a place for himself in society through the portals of religion and gradually managed to get a small foothold on the political platform also. Once there, he got addicted to the idea of controlling others.

Caught in the manoeuvres of political competition, he was no longer the gregarious fellow of earlier days. To a certain extent his personality had become overshadowed by feelings of jealousy. Instead of praising others, he enjoyed hearing himself being praised.

Since the time his daughter had married a white man, Gajjan Singh had broken off all relations with her. But his wife, being after all a mother, would occasionally visit her daughter without telling her husband.

There was constant tension and fear in the family, lest the other children become disobedient, too. But, their younger daughter understood her mother's predicament and would often try and comfort her. Their son had got a job in the United States and visited home twice or thrice a year, though it was quite some time back since he had last visited. The younger son was studying in the University of Warwickshire, and was away from home.

Whenever Gajjan Singh would get angry, he would

blame his wife for everything. Had he been in India, he would also have probably slapped her in anger. England had at least made him change in this matter. He had to change; otherwise the family would have disowned him. Gurmeet Kaur, too, had changed; she was no longer frightened by his bouts of rage.

In fact, at times she would even retort that he never spared any time for his own children since he was always busy directing others.

Maybe, it was the heartache caused by her daughter's action that had made Gurmeet physically weak. She hardly stepped out of her home. After her son's wedding, people rarely saw her going out for shopping.

Gajjan Singh did not get along with his children and daughter-in-law. Although he was no longer the gurdwara president, he had not shed his habit of acting as president at home. Gurmeet Kaur had suffered him all her life stoically, but his children refused to tolerate such behaviour. Gajjan Singh had begun to feel very dispirited and lonely within. At times he could not understand what had gone wrong with him.

About six months after the marriage of their younger daughter, Gurmeet Kaur suddenly died of a heart attack. For Gajjan Singh staying at home was worse than being inside a prison. He even stopped calling his friends over. He would not sit with his son and daughter-in-law to watch TV or discuss anything. If in a genial mood, he would play with his grandson. Usually, he would be in such a mood only in the evening, after filling up a jug of water from the bathroom tap and taking it into his bedroom. He had started keeping a bottle and a glass in his bedroom now.

He did not much enjoy going to the gurdwara either. Neither was he happy at home. In order to have a change and to consign his wife's ashes into the sacred river, he got his tickets booked for India.

Starting from Delhi right up to his village there were police pickets at every step. Irritated and worried, afraid and apprehensive, Gajjan Singh reached his village at last. All streets were empty, all doors closed. Why was the village looking so desolate? He could not help recalling that earlier there was always a hustle and bustle on the streets until nine in the evening.

Neither were there men sitting, gossiping under the banyan tree, nor was a soul to be seen in other usual meeting places of the village. Lying in his upper-floor room, Gajjan Singh wondered, *How can one meet and share his suffering with his friends in a situation like this.*

There were hardly any men to be seen in the panchayat hall of the village governing body. Earlier, whenever he stepped out to take a round of the fields, he was greeted with, 'nice to see you Gajjan Singh' or 'when did you arrive, Englandian?' type of greetings. Now his ears yearned to hear that. He returned home even more dejected. He felt that not just his family members but also the entire village was upset with him.

Most of his peers and acquaintances were already dead. Their grown-up children had moved over to other places both within and outside India. Those who had not been able to move out had not survived due to either drugs or poverty. The third generation did not even know who Gajjan Singh was.

If one visits regularly, once every two or three years, then contact with one's fellow villagers is maintained. But this was Gajjan Singh's third visit in so many decades. The first time he had come here it had been only for three weeks. Of that, he along with his children, had spent just four or five days in the village. That was not enough time to renew one's contacts. The second time he had fallen ill after arrival and that had been a rather unpleasant experience.

Very soon, Gajjan Singh got tired of the village, too, and booked his return flight.

Sitting in the gurdwara, he told his friends about the situation in India, 'I must say India is in a bad shape. We are lucky here; we can leave the glass windows open and snore in peace. In India, people bolt even their grilled windows. The slightest noise in the street makes people wake up in alarm, and then they are unable to go back to sleep. Some keep awake but stay still, lest others should come to know that they are afraid. People bolt their doors as soon as the sun sets. There is fear and terror on the streets. People are robbed by the police as well as the robbers. At times, the robbers even kill. Now, it seems people are wary of the militants also. It is said that this is the reason why the militant movement has failed. Many bad elements had joined the movement, and brought a bad name to everyone.'

'Gajjan Singh, these killings are not by the boys of the Khalistan movement. The government is behind these. If the government wishes, this bloodshed can stop at once. Who knows how many policemen or government agents have infiltrated the movement!'

'I am not saying that your facts are wrong. I am merely saying that our information, sitting here, is based on the news we get through the papers. But people living in India have a better idea about what is actually happening.'

'I think your views have changed after visiting India,' said one of them.

'In order to stay there, he had to change his views. Otherwise, he would have been killed there,' said Balbir in jest causing mild laughter among the listeners.

'I am, what I have always been and shall remain the same. Time and circumstances change a man and it is but natural that the views, too, change with time. Indira Gandhi attacked the Golden Temple. I wrote resolutely against this misdeed in the papers. Whether she committed this sacrilege herself, or at the behest of her advisors, is immaterial. But I did not distribute sweets like you to celebrate her assassination. I want to follow the tenets of *Gurbani*.'

'Do you think there is no chance of the formation of Khalistan now? Maybe, one could grab a ministerial berth in case Khalistan were to come into existence,' said Balbir, laughing loudly along with his friend.

'Pose this question to your nephew. He is the leader of the Khalistanis these days. Even the gurdwara is under his group's possession,' an irritated Gajjan Singh replied to Balbir.

'One of my relatives had to shift from Delhi and is now living in Punjab,' Gajjan Singh continued. 'He was very distraught and probably rightly, too. He was telling me that we, the British passport holders, love Punjab beyond all bounds. "Bravo!" But he said the word in a tone that made it sound like "shame on you". He was saying that our boundless love for Punjab had taken its toll on his son and grandsons' lives. Then he began to cry inconsolably. I had no words for him. If one of you has, please go and explain that to him.'

For a while everyone became silent as they pondered over this poignant tale.

'It is quite clear that everything was well planned. The Congress Party hired goondas from Haryana and slaughtered Sikhs in Delhi in broad daylight. Even the Moguls did not do such a thing,' said an old man shifting from the bench to a chair.

'At places nature is the cause of suffering, and at other places it is man himself. Looks like the world is passing through inauspicious times. Did you hear that recently in China, many young men and women were run over by tanks on the orders of the government? On the one hand people are destroying walls like the Berlin wall and getting reunited, while on the other many more walls are being raised to create new divisions.'

'The day Rajiv Gandhi was killed, I was sitting in the library with Udham Singh. We were worried, lest some Sikh organisation should take the responsibility of having a hand behind the killing. That could have led to the slaughter of Sikhs outside Punjab once again. One spark of that kind leads to an uncontrollable fire. That is how politicians play their games,' said Karam Singh of Bilga village addressing Balbir.

'Karam Singh, what you say is right. These people are not bothered about what happens to the others as long as their own house remains intact,' said Udham Singh.

'The world is passing through calamitous times, indeed. Last week one hundred and twenty-five thousand people died in Bangladesh in a cyclone. We had never heard of such disasters earlier.'

'Udham Singh, but earlier we did not have television either. The entire village used to have one radio for all. No papers ever reached our villages in those days. Now, you get the news, complete with pictures, of anything happening anywhere in the world within five minutes.'

'But now even an eight- or nine-year-old knows more than what we knew at the age of forty. Now it is difficult for the mother to argue with her all-knowing child.'

'That is quite true,' many voices assented in unison.

Chapter Nineteen

Smith and Hunter was a very large company manufacturing aeroplane engines, tractors, trucks, cranes, cars and coaches.

Jagir Singh had been working in one of the units of this company for more than twenty-eight years. Initially, he had had to undertake very strenuous jobs. But there was no other option at that time as jobs were difficult to come by, and people remained unemployed for months on end. Those who lived with their relatives were lucky to get some affection and encouragement from them, but the ones who were alone in England were merely objects of pity for the others.

In the early days, most of the people arriving from India were illiterate labourers. They were happy even to get arduous, dirty and sweaty jobs in the foundries; jobs that were being discarded by the whites in favour of better and easier work. Gradually, Indian workers filled up all such vacancies. At that time, the Indian workers were not lazy and inactive like the present generation. In fact, they were known to be hard-working and diligent.

Maybe that is why in those days Indians were looked down upon by the whites as poor, and treated disdainfully. But today things have changed radically. Asians run their own businesses; their entire families work hard together. They keep their shops open on all seven days of the week. That is the reason they have been more successful than the whites.

In the residential areas, the whites may not like the dark faces who run these corner shops, but they cannot deny their usefulness either. They are able to buy grocery at odd hours and at short notice, if needed. Goods bought at large food marts do not always last the entire week. Some item or the other, be it bread, eggs, milk, sugar or toilet paper, runs short at the wrong time. That is why there is a need to go to these corner shops even on Sundays.

Those days, Balbir Singh used to work with Jagir Singh. One day, he voiced his ideas to Jagir Singh, 'Look at the Moslems, they have managed to secure a room for saying their prayers. We can also get a separate room for Sikh religious activities, if we try.'

'Balbir Singh, what is the use of getting a room? Are we going to read scriptures there?'

'But, my friend, we can keep books, films and tapes related with our religion in that room. Many will benefit from such a library.'

During lunch break, Ravinder also came and sat next to them with his cup of tea. When they sought Ravinder's opinion on the matter he replied, 'Friends, this is a factory and we come here to work. Whatever you propose to do in that room is already being taken care of by the gurdwaras.

'Do you remember the days when we did not even have proper toilets in the factories? There were no proper arrangements to protect us from the cold in winter. We managed somehow at that time. The whites used to pity us. Do you remember the days when we used to belch loudly in the pubs and did not understand why the white man standing next to us looked at us as if we had vomited? We did not know what "manners" were, having come from villages. Now the whites are envious of the Mercedes cars our children drive, but cannot do anything about it or say anything.

'Consider this incident of yesterday. Patel had been feeling that the foreman always assigned him heavier tasks. He went to the union and squealed against the foreman saying that he discriminates against non-whites. Now, you tell me, do you think Nick is that sort of a person? He wants that the work should get done and admires a good worker. He is not bothered about the colour of his skin. If one of us were to become the foreman, probably we'll also behave in the same way. I am sorry, I've digressed. I am merely saying that we come here to work; let us not get into unnecessary complications. These are my personal views. You may do whatever you wish, but I am not interested in getting into this.'

They kept quiet for a while after hearing Ravinder. Then Jagir Singh said, 'I think he is right. We have three foremen in the assembly plant – Akhtar, Sharma and Dhanjal. If not all, most of the whites try and cooperate with them, while Asian workers are always looking for ways to pull them down. They always complain that they make no concessions for people of the same skin colour as theirs. They do not realise that these men are doing their job in a responsible manner, because that is what they are paid for. I think our compatriots are getting lazier day by day. They are ready to put in endless overtime provided there is no work to do. Sometimes they ask why we should work hard, when the whites do not. We think everyone who is white is also English. But even among the whites there are many who have arrived from faraway places.'

Sensing a kind of consensus in their views, Balbir said, 'Maybe, what you say is right. But earlier we did not have any organisation to go to for redressal. We did not know the language in order to understand them or make ourselves understood. But now we have our own governing bodies. We must make use of those.'

'Yes, we must make use of them, but not in a wrong way.'

'Isn't that human nature that a man wants to sit comfortably as soon as he is given a foothold?'

'Well, our folks have not been very upright either. They indulged in tax evasion soon after arriving here. They gave

111

false names to pass off other people's children as their own. Sisters called their brothers, fiancés. Even now, many of us are fleecing the government. Many of us are working, and still taking unemployment allowance. These are the types that shout the most, "The English have exploited and looted us." Someone should ask them a simple question – isn't it true that their educated children are earning salaries like forty thousand pounds per annum? And, still they say that England has given them nothing.'

'But the English plundered India for decades. The massacre at Jallianwala Bagh...'

'Balbir Singh, had you been the ruler, you would have done the same. Had it been Iran, France or Germany instead of England, they would have been no different. Besides, we cannot always revert to this single argument against the English.

'You have turned the conversation in a completely different direction. I wanted to tell you how the brother-in-law of Mr Sharma got a compensation of ten thousand pounds. He had complained against the high-handedness of the manager. He said that he could not afford to leave his job as his family was completely dependent on him. But the behaviour of his manager caused him acute stress and he had started suffering from high blood pressure. Since, we have such agencies now to back us up, we must make use of those. If he had not managed to arrive here, in England, and stayed in India, do you think he could have managed such a thing?'

'But it is not just our people; whites too indulge in similar hanky-panky. So do people from other countries. Whosoever gets a chance to fleece, fleeces,' Balbir said with some irritation.

'You are right, Balbir Singh. What you are saying is true. But, let us go. It is time to resume work.'

Chapter Twenty

When Sohan had been shifted to the testing section and began to work there, he had become very friendly with his co-worker, John. They were often together during the tea breaks, too. Gradually, their friendship led to closer social interaction between them beyond their working hours, or alternately one may say that their closeness had turned into real friendship. John and his wife Lisa, had danced the bhangra, with zeal, at Sohan's party. But after Sohan left that job, he lost contact with John, too. For many years now, Sohan had seen neither John nor Lisa in the pub, which they all used to frequent earlier.

After many years, Sohan went to the same pub by the station. He had just got his glass filled at the counter, and had barely taken a sip, when he spotted John sitting in a corner. John was sitting all by himself, looking forlorn and depressed. John sipped some beer from his glass, and got engrossed in the paper in front of him. Sohan knew that John always drank bitter.

Sohan emptied the glass in his hand, got two more filled with bitter and brought them to John's table. Seeing Sohan, John immediately perked up, shook hands with him and asked, 'Long time no see, my friend. How's life treating you?'

'I am fine, John. Tell me, how are you?' He sat down facing John.

'I am all right. I work for an insurance company. The salary is good and so is the atmosphere. Life is going on.'

They chatted for quite some time. As soon as their glasses were drained, John went to the counter and got them refilled; he also brought two packets of crisps from there. Noticing a shadow of despondency on John's face, and entries marked on the 'Soulmates' column of the newspaper, Sohan Singh finally decided to ask, 'How is Lisa doing, John? Did you have another child after Nikki?'

'Mr Singh, we have been out of touch for years. But you know all about my private life. We are old friends, so why should I hide anything from you? Lisa and I broke up long time ago.

'Actually, she fell in love with someone at her workplace. Maybe I had something lacking in me which Lisa found in him. He is a very nice man, indeed. Lisa and I stayed separately for a year and then finally divorced. You know that Lisa is a bit short-tempered, and most of the time she does what she thinks is best for her.

'They had invited me over to their home last Christmas. Mr Leach is a very nice man. He loves Nikki like his own daughter. But it is Lisa who, at times, disturbs the peace of the household and turns it into a battle of wits. Whether it is about selecting the right shade of wallpaper for the room, or about choosing an indoor plant; or about where to place the sofa and where to keep the plants; or about the colour and design of the curtains – Lisa must have everything her way. She insists that her choice must become the other person's choice, too.

'That night, after returning from their party I kept thinking of Lisa for a long time. Then I invited them over for the new year's party. I should not even call that a party as I had not invited anyone else except them. Actually, I was worried about Lisa. I live in a council flat in Rush Green. I have given my house to Lisa for the sake of Nikki's future. Please come over sometime. Take down my phone number and address.'

Then he resumed his conversation again, 'Mr Leach is a good-hearted gentleman with no vices. It is very difficult to live alone. Maybe that is why Mr Leach puts up with Lisa's tantrums. I do not want that after breaking up our relationship Lisa should once again undergo a break up with Mr Leach. If she leaves Michael Leach, she'll be sorry for the rest of her life. When I see her happy with Michael, I feel happy, too. But now I keep worrying that she may ruin her life due to these minor irritants.

'Mr Singh, if possible, you should also make her see sense. Do make an effort and meet her under some pretext or the other.'

Noticing that tears had welled up in Sohan Singh's eyes, John asked with some amazement, 'What is the matter, Mr Singh? Are you unwell or have you turned emotional?'

Taking John's hand in his own and pressing it, Sohan Singh merely uttered, 'John, you are great.'

That night Sohan Singh kept thinking of John for a long time. He could not go off to sleep until he had shared everything he had heard from John with his wife, Nirmala.

The following day when Nirmala shared this with Paramjit and Sarla, they were deeply moved.

'In spite of differences these people are still caring. They do not want to destroy either someone else's life or their own.'

'That is true, they also value life. Remember that old man Milkha Singh? The one who was kicked out of his home by his son and daughter-in-law after his wife died?'

'Yes, yes. I see him often near the gate of the park, with a can of beer in his hand.'

'Yes, the same fellow. One day he had a heart attack and fell down by the roadside. Our folks went past him without even bothering to find out what had happened. They presumed that he must have had too much to drink. Then a white couple came, got out of their car and shook him. By then he was already unconscious. They were the ones who called for the ambulance and made arrangements to get him to the hospital. He would have otherwise died lying there.'

'In India one does not call the police or take an injured man to the hospital, afraid of the possible police harassment later, but there is no instance of that in this country. Then why be afraid?'

'The police here are very nice, indeed. The other day we were returning from *Bhaji's* house and the motorway was totally jammed. Balwinder left the motorway and took a smaller countryside road instead. It was night and was snowing also. The visibility was poor and we got stuck in a place, making it impossible to get the car out. Meanwhile, it began to snow heavily. We were extremely worried until the time the police came and relieved us. We knew that they would see to it that we reach somewhere safe. On the contrary, if you find yourself in a similar situation in India and the police arrive, it is a cause for worry. Their tendency is to search your vehicle to find an excuse to extract money from you. That is why, because of all such conveniences here, everyone wants to come to these countries, to settle down here by hook or by crook.'

'Nirmala, you won't believe this. When I visited India last time, I had gone to the bank to withdraw some money. Half a day was wasted there. I was going to withdraw my own money but they behaved as if I had come asking for a bank loan to be sanctioned. An unnecessarily huge staff was present at the bank. Someone was sipping tea, someone was busy chatting while someone else was busy calling up his home. There was no one to serve the clients.

'But here, just one girl at the counter deals with the queue of customers. No one has to wait for more than a minute, and at times even less than that.'

Chapter Twenty One

Mindo had returned from India just a week ago. She called up Baldev from Newcastle. '*Bhaji*, *Bhapaji* has sent you the message that he is no longer in a position to travel to England. His knees give him a lot of trouble. He joked that in his old age, he has to pay for all those thousand sit-ups he used to do at one go when he was young. *Bibi* also doesn't keep good health. They have asked you to go and visit them. Moreover, they have not met the children for years now. And yes, there is one more matter *Bhaji*. The son of the Dolike family had gone on a visit to India from Canada, and asked for his share of land from his brothers. Believe it or not, they were ready to cut each other upon this issue. Going by such incidents, I suggest that you should go and finalise the division of our ancestral land. *Bhapaji* has also suggested the same.'

'Mindo, maybe you are not aware of all the facts. The Dolike family had spent three lakh rupees from the joint household income to send that son to Canada. Three lakh rupees in those days is equal to seven lakh rupees in today's terms, maybe even more. With that money any of the three brothers could have gone to Canada. The three brothers have just ten acres of land. Once in Canada, this fellow never sent a penny back home. I doubt whether he sent money to his wife. Then how can he ask for his share in the ancestral land? Or he should be ready to share his property in Canada with his brothers. Only then he can rightfully stake his claim in the property back home.'

'But *Bhaji*, everyone does not think as you do. Neither the ones living there, nor the ones who live here.'

'First of all, Mindo, our children are not going to return

to India and till the land. True, that at times your sister-in-law and I do think that after retirement we may go and spend four or five months there every year.

'If *Bhaji* and his children act wisely, that is, if they keep the people who visit them from England, happy and make them feel wanted, then they can keep everything. But even if they do not behave well, I am not going to keep all five acres that belong to me. I'll merely keep half of that to indulge in gardening and to rear cattle if I want to. The house is big enough to accommodate everyone. In fact, your sister-in-law...'

'But *Bhaji*, wherever one lives, one has to fend for oneself. Ajit *Bhaji* does not interfere in anything now. His sons and their wives do not think that it is necessary to take his advice. Times have changed. It is the same story everywhere. Nobody wants to work; everyone dresses up and watches TV. Or people pick up their motorbikes and scoot away. The hard work is left to the *bhayyas*; it is up to them whether they work or not.

'Throughout our stay, we brought grocery for ourselves from the city and kept it in the kitchen. The entire family was always ready to go for a drive in our jeep, or to go and drink beer and eat meat in the restaurants on our account. Pappu's father would bring meat, sweets, beer and whisky everyday from the city. You should have seen how everyone would gather near him like flies on a piece of jaggery. Our folks in India now keep wondering what we will gift them when they come to visit us or what we will take for them, when we go to visit them.'

Both of them began to laugh at this statement.

'All right, give the phone to my sister-in-law. Let me ask her how she is...'

Baldev kept on turning the pages of his life for a long while. How sweet was life in times bygone! How endearing was the innocence and simplicity of minds in those days! People were ready to sacrifice anything for the sake of friendship and kinship. People of a family cared for each other, notwithstanding the economic hardships. Neighbours could depend on their neighbours.

Similarly, it was always a great pleasure to chance upon someone in England who was from the same village.

He recalled the tales heard from O'Brian, who used to recount stories of the time before the advent of television. His stories would remind Baldev of his childhood and youth.

His neighbour O'Brian used to tell him that in those days they never bothered to lock their home. Baldev remembered that when he had first arrived in England the custom was to leave a pound note in an envelope under the empty milk bottle at the doorstep. The milkman would replace the bottle, take what was his due and leave the change in the same envelope in the postbox.

But now times had changed. Given a chance, someone might try and filch anything that was accessible. You could not trust people the way you did in those days.

The house that earlier seemed like a villa to Baldev, looked very small and old-fashioned to him during this trip to India. A lot of people had constructed elegant houses. In some of the porches one could also spot cars parked.

These beautiful houses, built on both sides of the peripheral road, had water tanks built on their rooftops. These tanks were of various shapes and designs; some were built like a flowerpot, while others resembled a car, a van, an aeroplane or a helicopter.

Going by the obvious opulence of his village, Baldev began to feel that his first requirement was a proper house. A house that could be spotted from afar like the newly built houses. And a house that would please his children whenever they visited India on a holiday.

He asked Kuku to mediate between him and Kehru the

junkie, as Baldev was interested in buying five hundred square yards of Kehru's land next to the peripheral road. After much negotiation Kehru agreed to sell the required area for three lakh rupees. Baldev immediately got the land registered in his name.

Paramjit was very happy. She too, yearned for a modern and beautiful house of their own. When he called Sohan and told him about the plans, his reply was that he should have added another three to four lakh rupees more and bought land in the city somewhere. That would have given them better resale value in case they wished to sell the property at a later stage.

But Baldev Singh's argument was that there was hardly any difference between urban and rural areas these days. In fact, the moneyed people from the cities preferred to construct their homes in colonies, reclaimed from farmland, outside the city suburbs.

'Well, if you are satisfied then I am satisfied too. I am happy for you Baldev Singh.' Sohan Singh concluded the argument.

Baldev Singh got the architectural plans sanctioned and started the construction of the three-bedroomed house. The bedrooms were on the upper floor; the master bedroom had an attached bathroom. The ground floor consisted of a hall, kitchen, dining room, veranda and a garage.

Once the construction started, Baldev Singh came back to England for a while. He would sit with his family and enthusiastically describe the design and the layout of their prospective home.

Everything had become very expensive and Baldev Singh ended up spending five to seven lakh rupees more than he had estimated earlier. He was impatiently awaiting the completion so that he could call Paramjit and buy the furniture with her help.

After that they would call their children over.

Chapter Twenty Two

It was a Saturday. Baldev and his wife, pushing their baggage trolley, had barely reached the ground level from the car park of terminal three at Heathrow when they spotted Ravinder with an elderly couple beside him. They met, hugged each other and enquired after each other's well-being.

Baldev had come to see his wife off, while Ravinder was there to send his in-laws. In a few minutes, Ravinder's wife also joined them. Soon she and Paramjit were chatting away.

Baldev and Ravinder were meeting after a long time. At one time they had lived in the same area in East London. But Ravinder had shifted to Reading many years ago and later bought a wine shop there. It was a nice coincidence that Ravinder's in-laws and Paramjit were going to India by the same flight.

After the three passengers disappeared into the departure hall, Ravinder and his wife insisted that Baldev should visit their home before returning to London.

Getting out of the car park, Ravinder asked Baldev to follow his car. If they get separated, he should wait for him at the first petrol station after exiting the motorway.

At Ravinder's house, they kept talking until sunset. Eventually, Ravinder and his wife persuaded Baldev to spend the night at their place and go home in the morning. Baldev called home to tell his children that he would return the following day.

It was around seven in the evening, when Baldev and Ravinder came to the nearby pub called Sand and Sea.

They sat reminiscing over beer. They talked about the jobs in the earlier days, the low cost of grocery in those times, the simplicity of the people then, the ease with which white girls could be hooked, and the great advantage people fluent in English had over the others. They also talked about their initial struggle after reaching England, about the life back home, the politics there, about lovers lost and now forgotten, and about farms, crops and wells they had left behind. They were so engrossed in randomly turning the pages of their lives that they did not realise how time had ticked away until it was already eleven o'clock.

When they came out of the pub, their conversation drifted to Ravinder's in-laws.

'You haven't told me for how long your mummy and daddy were here?' Baldev asked.

'My friend, I thought of them as Mummy and Daddy, but they are the ones who forced me to consider them as in-laws. At times even my wife gets upset with me over the issue.'

'Stop talking in riddles. Tell me the story straight.'

'Well, my wife had been nagging me for quite some time; she was very keen about her *bibi* and *bhapa's* visit to England. So, we invited them over. My wife insisted that we must give them the room above the stairs. There was a lot of junk lying in that room, which I removed to the garage and redecorated the room. We also had a new carpet for the room.

'The day her mummy and daddy landed here, the mother slept in our bedroom with her daughter and I with *Bhapa* in the adjoining room. The following day my wife told her *bibi*, "Here is your room, *Bibi*. Both of you may sleep here."

'"And where are you sleeping?" her mother asked.'

High on beer, sometimes he referred to her as Mummy, sometimes as *Bibi*. Actually, Ravinder's wife used to call her mother *Bibi* in India, but after reaching England she had adopted the more fashionable form of address 'Mummy'.

'My wife replied, "I'll sleep in the room where we had slept last night."

'"And your *bhapa*, where is he going to sleep?"

'"He'll also sleep here. This room is for both of you."

'*Bibi* jumped from the bed as if hit by something and said, "Don't you have any shame left? We did not sleep together when it was time to sleep together. I am not going to sleep with him in the same room now. I am going to sleep with you in your room where we had slept last night, even if I have to sleep on the floor."

'The old man said, "It is up to you; whatever is convenient to you, or is the custom here. I'll sleep wherever you'll ask me to sleep."'

'Then, what happened?'

'What could have happened? After about ten days and much cajoling the old lady agreed to sleep in that room. But the old man had to be shifted to the back room. Our children came visiting us during one of the weekends. They had a real good laugh when we told them this story.'

They kept talking till late in the night after returning home. Baldev said, 'Let me tell you an incident about a relative of one of my friends. He had also invited his father-in-law over. The old man was known to be an opium taker in India. My friend thought that the stay in England would probably de-addict him. When he was leaving for the pub, his wife said, "Please take *Bhapa* also to the pub and show him around. *Bhapa* has started taking beer now."

'So, my dear fellow, urged by his wife took his father-in-law to the pub. After consuming two glasses of beer the old man asked, "Where is the urinal here?" My friend took him to the toilet and told him that he could stand there and pee. The old man was wearing a pyjama under his trousers and could not untie the cord. The men standing behind began to enjoy this strange scene. Finally, my friend lost his temper and said to his father, "What is this scene you are creating here? Go inside the cubicle and bolt it from inside. Then you can untie your cord at leisure. People standing here are already laughing at you."

'My friend told me that when the old man returned after a while, he was smelling of phenol and said, "These white people are idiots. They have kept small soap bars against the wall where people pee. So, I took those out. I have also washed my face and hands. This soap has a smell but does not lather." Exasperated, my friend took the old man home and never took him to the pub again. Instead, he would bring a bottle for him to be consumed at home.'

'Yes, there are some old people like that. But, a lot of spice is added by the raconteurs also.'

'In earlier days, people had to be told how to use a toilet seat. But now… now they learn everything in India itself.'

Chapter Twenty Three

Ever since Paramjit and Baldev had visited India, Nirmala had become hell-bent on buying a house there. She would remind Sohan every now and then, 'You have not yet seen the video film of Paramjit's house. When you see it, you'll also want to buy a house immediately. All their relatives gathered on the day their new home was completed, for the recital from the holy book. You could see on the video how proudly Baldev *Bhaji* was walking around. These are the kind of things that add to a man's stature.'

'I have seen that film in Baldev Singh's house, even before you saw it. The only part I did not get to see was the shots of the celebrations when everyone danced the *giddha* and bhangra. You may not want to believe me, but let me tell you, they will not visit that house more than three or four times. Then they'll get weary of travelling all the way to India. After that happens, who knows if someone will stay in that house or it will remain empty! Baldev Singh himself used to advise Kailay Sahib, "What is the point in building a house in Jawahar Nagar. No one will have the time to travel so far." But at that time Kailay Sahib had not paid heed to him. I hear that now Kailay Sahib is interested in selling that house.'

'If Kailay *Bhaji* is selling his house, why not buy it from him? Please find out how much is he selling it for?'

'I had even told Baldev Singh not to construct a house. However, since his pockets are brimming now, he did not listen to me. And now you are running doggedly after a house. Like others, you too will get weary of this expensive fetish soon.'

Sohan Singh was not in favour of buying a house.

'Can I say something if you promise not to get irritated? Please hear me out attentively,' Nirmala said and began looking at Sohan Singh expectantly.

'What is that gem of an idea you have that I should hear you out attentively?'

'I have found out from Sarla that they are selling the house. Both of us have seen that house. It is a very nice and commodious house. It is also well located. We may have to merely change the flooring. Or maybe, even that can wait. For the time being we may just change the flooring in the hall and the veranda. Terrazzo flooring is considered old-fashioned nowadays; we'll change that to marble. Otherwise that house is excellent. If at all, we may need to get it repainted. There is a very nice garden in the front and also at the back. Please find out at what price do they wish to sell it. I have also found out that they are interested in getting paid in England in pounds. It is possible that the deal will work out cheaper for us this way.' Nirmala was impatient to buy a house.

When Sohan Singh told Baldev Singh about this proposal, he had a good laugh and said, 'I could never have imagined that the man who used to advise others against buying a house in India will one day get tempted into buying one for himself.'

He began to laugh again and then asked, 'Shall I give my considered opinion?'

'Of course, my friend. Stop confusing me further and just tell me what should I do?'

'What is there to be done? Go ahead and please your wife; jump into the fire for her sake,' replied Baldev.

'So, you mean I should go ahead and clinch the deal?' Sohan Singh tried to gauge whether Baldev was serious.

'You know that all of us have been chasing some dream or the other throughout our lives. Life is for dreaming. For some, their dreams come true, for the others they remain mere dreams. We are the lucky ones who have seen most of our dreams come true. Maybe that is why we still feel young and energetic like a healthy horse. There is another thing to be kept in mind. We had left our families behind and had to send money home for their sustenance and to put them on a firm footing. Besides, we had to buy homes here and educate our children. But our children are free from similar concerns. Then why must we worry about our children unnecessarily?

'You have some money saved. You are not going to take that with you to the other world. If you buy a house, that would remain here. If you put the money in a bank, that, too, will stay here. How does it matter if your children inherit a little more or a little less from you? They are not going to reward you for your generosity; in any event, you won't even be there to receive anything. Who knows how the ones we'll leave behind will think of us? Who will remember us with gratitude and who with mere disdain?

'Let the children live the way they want to, and try and fulfil Nirmala's and your desires before you die. If along with Nirmala, your children are also in favour of buying a house, then it is even better. Kailay Sahib would sell it cheap now. So, go ahead and take the plunge without weighing the pros and cons endlessly. And who knows, maybe occasional visits to India will make the post-retirement life more colourful. Remember that couplet of poet Sahir? "Live in such a way that..."'

Baldev met Kailay Sahib over the weekend and finalised everything.

The same evening they gathered in Sohan Singh's home to celebrate. To them, it seemed as if the purpose of life was to help each other, nurture friendships and relationships, and enjoy each other's company.

Encouraged by this easy and friendly atmosphere, the children playing around them were also feeling more free and unconstrained and were jumping joyously.

Time was moving at its pace, oblivious of everything.

Sohan Singh searched for the same song and began to play it: 'Live in such a way that...'

Glossary

Anand Karaj	Religious part of a marriage ceremony
Babaji	Grandfather
Babuji	A respectful title or form of address for a man, especially an educated one
Bahenji	Sister
Bapu	Father
berseem	Greens for cattle
Bhabi	Sister-in-law
Bhaji	Brother/brother-in-law
Bhapa	Father/father-in-law
bhayya	Labourer from the Indian states of Bihar and UP
Bibi	Mother
chadra	A garment worn chiefly in rural areas
chamar	Person belonging to a lower caste
chhimbas	A low caste usually in the profession of tailoring
giddha	Folk dance of Punjab performed by women
Granthi	Priest
Gurbani	Contents of the holy book of Sikhs
Jatta	Man belonging to the farming class
Jatti	Woman belonging to the farming class
Jutt	A person belonging to the north-western part of India engaged mainly in agriculture
Khalistan	Name given by Sikh nationalists to a proposed independent Sikh state
langar	Food that is served free of cost at a Sikh temple
Maji	Mother/mother-in-law

masoor	A lentil of a small orange-red variety
mems	White-skinned foreigners (ladies)
papad	A large circular piece of thin, spiced bread made from ground lentils and fried in oil
Pitaji	Father
ruri	Manure
subedar	A sergeant in the army
Taya	Uncle, elder brother of father
Tayee	Aunt, wife of father's elder brother
Wahe Guru	An expression of salutation to the supreme Lord in Sikhism